Strangers in the LAND

Strangers in the LAND

REVIEW AND HERALD® PUBLISHING ASSOCIATION
Since 1861 | www.reviewandherald.com

Copyright © 1964 by Review and Herald® Publishing Association

Published by Review and Herald® Publishing Association, Hagerstown, MD 21741-1119

Review and Herald® titles may be purchased in bulk for educational, business, fund-raising, or sales promotional use. For information, e-mail SpecialMarkets@reviewandherald.com.

The Review and Herald® Publishing Association publishes biblically based materials for spiritual, physical, and mental growth and Christian discipleship.

The author assumes full responsibility for the accuracy of all facts and quotations as cited in this book.

This book was
Cover designed by Trent Truman
Cover art by Clyde Provonsha/© Review and Herald® Publishing Association
Typeset: Bembo 12/15

PRINTED IN U.S.A.

13   12   11   10   09   5   4   3   2   1

Library of Congress Cataloging-in-Publication Data

Vernon, Louise A., 1914-2001
    Strangers in the Land / Louise A. Vernon
        126 p. illus. 22 cm.
    1. Huguenots—History—Juvenile literature.
I. Title.
    PZ7.V598 St
    3245861 (OCoLC)
            64017651

ISBN 978-0-8280-2426-6

Contents

CHAPTER 1

Midnight Meeting

The peal of church bells shattered the noonday stillness of La Rochelle, a seaport town in France. Townspeople listened with astonishment. Some frowned and looked frightened. Others smiled and nodded their heads in satisfaction.

In the bakery shop the baker shook his head and crossed himself before he put the swelling loaves in the ovens to bake. Next door the cobbler sat openmouthed, his hammer raised over the upturned shoe on his last. Across the town square the tax collector straightened up from his account books, chuckled, and rubbed his palms together. In a stone building not far away the Huguenot pastor turned pale and dropped to his knees in prayer.

The bells kept pealing.

At the port, where a ship had just arrived, the longshoremen stopped their unloading to listen. Surprise and alarm showed on their faces.

Inside a walled garden on the outskirts of La Rochelle, Pierre Le Brun and his 7-year-old brother Henri heard the bells and stopped building their mud fort. Their mother, Madame Le Brun, ran from the house, and clasped Henri to her.

Frightened by her strained look, Pierre whispered, "Is there danger?"

His mother silenced him with pursed lips.

"Mother," Pierre's little brother asked, "why are the bells ringing at this time of day?"

A tear rolled down Madame Le Brun's face. Henri, with a puzzled look, brushed it off with his forefinger.

"Mother, don't cry. What is there to cry about? I haven't been naughty, have I?"

"No, no. Of course not, my darling." Madame Le Brun took a deep breath.

Little Henri stared at her. "Why do the bells keep ringing?"

"I'm not exactly sure."

His mother's tone pierced Pierre with a nameless dread. What could the bells mean?

Before he could ask more, a tiny, wiry woman darted out of the house, wringing her hands. "Oh, madame, I spilled the salt sack into the flour. Now they're both ruined. Oh, those bells— that's what did it. Something dreadful is going to happen. I just know it."

Mother would have to explain now, Pierre thought, but she remained calm.

"Now, Othalie, don't excite yourself like this, and don't throw out anything. The salt tax is very high this year. We'll just use the flour and salt together for cooking. I'll send Pierre to the baker's for bread." She smiled a little. "Or perhaps you'd rather go."

Othalie blushed. "Madame mustn't tease me. I have too much to do in the house. Besides, he's coming to see me tonight." She fled with a flutter of her long skirts.

Mother gave Pierre some coins. "One loaf will be enough, Pierre, and if there's any news about—about anything, listen carefully."

Pierre ran almost all the way to the town square. At the baker's shop he found the door locked. Perplexed, he cupped his hands and peered through the window. The counters inside were bare. He knocked on the door several times, but no one came.

Pierre remembered a side door that led to the huge brick ovens. As he approached, the door opened a crack. The plump baker, Alec Calvet, looked out, a finger to his lips. He motioned Pierre inside.

Trays of fresh bread stood on wooden worktables. The massive ovens, still hot from the baking, sent out waves of warm air. The delicious fragrance of the loaves made Pierre's mouth water.

"Mother wants a loaf of bread," Pierre said. "Is there some reason you closed your shop, Alec?"

For answer the baker thrust a long, crusty loaf of bread into Pierre's hands. "You haven't heard?" He frowned a little. "Well, then, I'll let your parents tell you. It's a long story, all about you Huguenots."

"Does it have something to do with the church bells ringing?"

Alec Calvet sighed. "Yes, it does. Now run along. Don't let anybody see you if you can help it."

He opened the door and looked out over the square. "It's all right. No one's out there now. I guess everybody went home as soon as the news got around."

"What news?"

The baker pushed him out gently. "Ask your parents."

The bolt shot home behind Pierre. The town square looked larger than it ever had before. Even in the October sunlight the shadows from the overhanging apartments on the side streets loomed dark and menacing. Filled with a strange fear, Pierre ran home, not daring to look back. Out of breath, he arrived at the garden gate and pulled the bell rope three times, the Le Brun family's private signal. Othalie let him in.

"Any news?"

Pierre shook his head. What could he say? He hadn't found out anything yet. Then he heard his father's voice.

"Is Father home from the port already?" he asked.

Othalie nodded.

"But he never comes home this early," Pierre said.

He ran to find his father, but there was no sign of either him or his mother. Pierre stood perplexed in the hallway. From behind the closed bedroom door he heard the subdued voices of his parents. Pierre was more puzzled than ever. His parents had never shut out the family before.

A thump from the front room reminded him that Henri was hiding somewhere, ready for a game of hide-and-seek with his father.

Pierre waited a few minutes, hoping Father and Mother would come out and explain what was happening; but the bedroom door remained closed. Pierre called to his younger brother from the doorway, "Henri, come out. There won't be any hide-and-seek today."

At first he could see no movement anywhere in the room. Then the top of the carved window seat moved a fraction of an inch. The tip of Henri's nose appeared.

Pierre's uneasiness welled up into violent anger.

"Henri, don't ever hide in there again. It's dangerous. Don't you know you could suffocate?"

Stepping out, Henri ran his finger through a hole in the panel. "There's no lock. Air can go through that hole. How could I suffocate?"

"It's dangerous, I tell you." Pierre sounded cross.

"Where's Father?" Henri asked, looking past Pierre.

"He's talking to Mother. Let's go see what Othalie is cooking for supper."

In the kitchen the boys watched Othalie cube vegetables and put them in an iron kettle suspended in the fireplace. Pierre's uneasiness never left him, but somehow he could not bring himself to question Othalie about the church bells.

Later Othalie set the table for supper. "Where's madame tonight?" She stopped as if startled by the change of routine. "And monsieur? Supper is ready. Will you call them, Pierre, while I dip up the soup?"

Pierre tiptoed down the hall. He could not have explained why, except that the strange feeling enveloped him again. He called to his parents in a voice little more than a whisper. To his relief, they came out at once and went to the supper table.

Pierre looked forward to the usual laughter and happy talk after grace, but tonight grace itself was different. Father didn't even use the same words.

"Almighty God, our Father and Divine Protector, may this food replenish our strength that we may serve Thee as Thy soldiers, and defend Thy name against the enemies who now surround us."

His voice rang with passionate intensity as he went on. "May we strike down evil with Thy sword of truth. May we put on the armor of righteousness—"

He stopped with a suddenness that made Pierre look up. Mother had laid her hand on Father's arm.

"Amen," Father said.

Not another word was spoken during the meal. Even Henri kept quiet. Afterward Othalie scurried through her household chores, but this, Pierre reminded himself, was usual. Othalie entertained the baker, her husband-to-be, twice a week, and she always hurried on visiting nights.

But tonight was different. Alec Calvet had hardly come into

the house when Mother took him and Othalie aside, speaking in a low voice.

"Oh, Madame Le Brun, why didn't you say so?" Othalie said. "I would have had the house all ready. Alec, you will have to go. It will take half the night to clean up. I'll see you tomorrow." She urged the big man out. "Now," she said, "I'd better get into the front room. Oh, if madame had only told me."

Her actions puzzled Pierre. She got down on her hands and knees with scrubbing brush and bucket, and polished the already-clean hearthstone. The blaze from the fire and her exertions brought a flush to her face.

"But Othalie, you scrubbed it this morning." Pierre did not dare ask outright why she was cleaning house at night. Neither would he admit his fear of the changes taking place. Something sinister lurked in every corner.

"Do go away, Pierre; there's a good boy." Othalie rubbed her cheek.

Henri's bedtime came and went. Othalie did not come to get him ready. She kept running from front room to kitchen, dusting the spotless chairs, the huge spinning wheel, and the carved window seat.

"What is she doing that for?" Henri asked.

Pierre didn't know, but he wasn't going to admit his ignorance in front of his brother.

"Oh," he said in an airy voice, "we're going to have visitors." As soon as he said it, he knew it was true. But what visitors, and why?

The bell to the garden gate jangled.

"Maybe it's Grand-père." *(Grand-père is* French for grandfather.) Henri jumped up in excitement.

The bell rang again three times, evenly spaced.

"That's our ring, not Grand-père's. Somebody is coming. We'd better go upstairs, Henri."

When Othalie opened the front door, Pierre heard a man's voice murmuring. Strain as he would from the landing, he could not make out a word.

"Who is it, Pierre?" Henri asked.

"I can't tell. Come on, Henri. Let's go to bed."

"Are you going to bed when I do?" Henri appeared enchanted with the idea and undressed without protest.

He dropped off to sleep with startling suddenness, and Pierre was left staring up at the darkness, trying to make sense of the happenings downstairs. He heard the garden bell again, three long peals. This visitor spoke no louder than the one before. After a time the same thing happened again. Five times the bell rang, but at such long intervals, Pierre was sure it must be almost morning.

He drowsed in a half sleep, but when the bell rang for the sixth time, he sat up wide awake. He had to know what was going on. He wrapped himself in bedclothes and tiptoed to the carved chest standing in the upper hail, the one Father kept locked all the time and would never open.

Pierre perched cross-legged on top. From where he sat he could almost see into the living room, except for the man-high spinning wheel that stood in the way. As it was, he saw men's legs passing and repassing. Whoever the guests were, they couldn't sit still.

There was a hush. A man began to pray. Pierre recognized the voice of Pastor Foudray, the Huguenot preacher. With a feeling of relief, Pierre bowed his head. He liked the pastor, a calm, gentle man with quiet humor.

Pierre could not make out the words of the prayer, but he lifted his head when he heard the "Amen." A babble of voices reached his ears, and then a man's voice rang out.

"Is it rumor, or is it fact?"

This time Pierre recognized the voice of Dr. Maurice, the Huguenot physician, who had been forbidden to practice medicine because of his religion.

"My brethren," Pastor Foudray said in a firm voice, we must face the truth. The church bells we heard today rang the death knell of religious freedom in France."

Pierre puzzled over the meaning of Pastor Foudray's words. Everyone knew that Huguenots could not hold public office, but did the pastor mean they couldn't meet together anymore to read the Bible and sing hymns?

"It can't be true," Father said in an excited voice. "The Edict of Nantes is perpetual."

"Brother Le Brun," Pastor Foudray said, "we all know that the edict has been interpreted according to the letter, not the spirit, especially during the past four years. Why do we have to have burials at night, for example? Because the edict did not specifically state that we were to bury our dead in the daytime. No, my brethren, the letter of the law has killed the spirit. I have seen the signs of the coming conflict for a long time."

Dr. Maurice's voice rang out: "Why must we Huguenots always fight our own countrymen? Why are we treated as if we were strangers in the land? Now, as you know, since I can no longer practice medicine, I have turned to compiling our history. I suggest that we do as so many of our brethren have done."

A silence followed. Pierre held his breath so as not to miss the doctor's next words. But it was Pastor Foudray who spoke.

" 'When they persecute you in this city, flee ye into another,' " he quoted. "Do you mean we should emigrate?"

"Yes," Dr. Maurice said, a tremor in his cultivated voice. "There's England, hardly a stone's throw from us, or Switzerland.

But I have another country in mind. In fact, I have written to a friend in the colony of Boston, Massachusetts, asking about conditions there in America."

"America?" The word echoed from person to person.

Pierre heard a gasp from the lower hall. Someone downstairs was listening.

"Oh, madame, how does he dare speak of America? People are all slaves there, treated worse than cattle. It's worse than the West Indies—a living death, they say."

Mother spoke in a sharp whisper. "The West Indies, yes. Everyone knows about that. But who told you this nonsense about America? You know that monsieur has two fishing vessels going to Newfoundland all the time, and they don't bring back reports like that."

"Alec Calvet told me, madame. He says things have changed so much in the past five years that there's no telling what will happen after today. And madame—"

"Yes?"

"Alec wants me to marry him right away before—before something might prevent it."

"Why, Othalie, you didn't tell me that."

"No, I just couldn't, madame. There'll be problems, Alec being a Catholic."

"Othalie, we've discussed all that before."

"Yes, but things are different now."

"Listen, Othalie. Pastor Foudray is talking."

The pastor's clipped voice rang out with new depth. "I asked that we meet here tonight. You have known me many years now. You know I am not excitable by nature, but I want you to know that I am now gathering food and guns."

The talk became so excited that Pierre was afraid Henri

would wake up. Pierre huddled on the chest, dazed and frightened by the pastor's words.

"And I would like to know from each of you what arms you have at home, for we surely will have to defend ourselves sooner or later."

"I can tell you in just a moment." Father started up the stairs.

Pierre sprang from the chest and fled to his room. He hid behind the door and listened to his father unlocking the chest. He heard the rattling of metal on metal. Beyond question, the chest held guns.

In that moment Pierre knew what the church bells meant—war against the Huguenots.

CHAPTER 2

𝔄 𝔓𝔯𝔬𝔪𝔦𝔰𝔢 𝔑𝔬𝔱 𝔎𝔢𝔭𝔱

Father locked the chest and went downstairs. Pierre, behind the door, listened for a moment longer before going back to bed. Something touched his arm. Pierre whirled around. His 7-year-old brother Henri stood by him, rubbing his eyes. A blanket trailed behind him.

"Is it time to get up?"

"No, Henri." Pierre tucked his brother in bed and lay down himself. The voices downstairs drifted farther and farther away. The next he knew, Othalie was shouting, "Hurry and get dressed. Your father wants to see you and Henri before he goes to the port."

"Boys," Father said when Pierre and Henri came into the kitchen, "something happened yesterday. It's too long to explain, but I want you both to stay inside the garden. If any strangers ring, run into the house. You see, there may be some people who would like to take you away from us, especially Henri."

"Where would they take me?" Henri asked.

"To a convent school," Father said. "Pierre, you must always look out for Henri."

Pierre nodded. After Father left, the boys went to their mud fort in the garden. Pierre gave Henri some twigs.

"There's your army," he said. "First the pikemen, then musketeers and cavalrymen, and last the dragoons."

The boys set up two armies.

"The musketeers come ahead and fire and then go behind

the pikemen to reload," Pierre said, moving some of his stick soldiers. "And we have to have two rows of cavalrymen—one row fires, and then they reload while the other row fires. The dragoons are last. They can fight on horseback or on foot."

Horses' hoofs clattered on the cobbled street outside.

Henri looked up, wide-eyed with fright. Pierre tried to hide his own sudden fear. He soothed his little brother in a whisper.

"Maybe they won't stop here. They—" The words died on his lips. The horses had stopped at the gate.

Henri's eyes brimmed with tears as he looked up at Pierre. "Don't let them take me away. I don't want to go to a convent school." He started to run toward the house, but Pierre caught him by the arm.

"It's too late to hide in there. We're safer out here if they break the gate down." He looked around for a hiding place. It was no use to hide behind the scraggly bushes. An early cold spell had stripped them of their leaves. Pierre pulled Henri behind the fort.

The bell at the gate clanged once, twice. There was a pause, and then three quick peals blended together.

With a shout of joy Pierre jumped up. "Come on, Henri. There's nothing to be afraid of. That's Grand-père's own special ring."

The boys ran to open the gate. Pierre's delight turned to amazement. Instead of Grand-père's carriage, white horses, and men in livery bowing and opening the carriage door, the only people outside were a white-haired old man and a boy on two saddle horses. The man took off a large feathered hat and handed it to the boy as they dismounted. The boy, a peasant about Pierre's age, helped the old man fasten the buttons of his dark, knee-length cape, and then drew out a clean handkerchief from the big patch pocket for the old man to wipe his face.

"Grand-père!" Both boys flung themselves on their grandfather. "What happened? Where is your carriage? You've never come home on a horse before. We didn't know you at first."

In spite of a look of pain and worry, Grand-père smiled and hugged the boys. "Where is your mother?"

"Inside. She and Othalie are weaving a rug."

Grand-père motioned the peasant boy to follow him into the house. At the door the boy took off his wooden sabots and carried them under his arm.

Mother and Othalie sat in the sunshiny front room, braiding bits of dark-blue velvet and pale-pink cloth, just as they always did in the morning after the work was done. At the sight of Grand-père, Mother flushed with pleasure and stood up so suddenly that the strips of cloth fell to the floor. With a little cry Othalie knelt and began to pick them up.

Mother ran to Grand-père, both hands extended in welcome. "Father! This is a surprise."

Grand-père's mouth twisted into an odd expression.

"You've heard—?" Mother gazed up at him as if trying to read his face.

Grand-père did not answer right away. He caught her hands in his and bent to kiss them.

Mother called to Othalie. "Never mind picking up now, Othalie. Bring a chair for Father."

Othalie drew up a chair near the fireplace. "Shall I light the fire, madame?"

"No, it's too warm for that. Sit down, Father. Do I know this young boy?" She smiled at the peasant boy, who stood rubbing his hand on his full, skirtlike breeches.

"This is Claude Arnaud," Grand-père said. "His parents died last winter—scarlet fever. Claude is a great help to me." He put his arm around the boy. "I didn't want to bring any of the men because they may have to defend the estate." Grand-père stopped, as if he had said too much. "But don't worry, Mathilde. We haven't seen any soldiers yet."

Mother picked up a braid of cloth and bent over her work. "Has it come to that so soon, Father?"

"Yes."

"Pierre could take a message to Paul if you think it is advisable. It's only a 20-minute walk to the port."

Grand-père stared at a patch of sunlight on the floor. "It would be advisable. We must plan what to do."

"Very well. Pierre, go tell your father that Grand-père is here on horseback. Be sure to say it just like that"

"May I go?" Henri asked, running to his mother.

"No!" Grand-père exploded. Henri's lips quivered.

"Henri, don't you remember what Father said this morning?" Mother asked.

"Oh," Henri said. "Somebody might take me."

Grand-père looked surprised.

"We can't take chances, Father. Paul warned them this morning."

Grand-père nodded. "You're a good boy, Henri," he said, "and you too, Pierre. Run and tell your father to come home as soon as he can. Take Claude with you," he added. "He's never been in town before."

Pierre ran to get his wide-brimmed beaver hat. Claude stared at it and at Pierre's fine leather shoes.

"Would you like to come with me, Claude?"

Claude nodded and bowed to mother and Grand-père. Once outside, Claude put on his wooden sabots.

"Claude, why did Grand-père come this way? What's going to happen? Do you know?" Pierre asked as they walked along the sea wall.

20

Claude shook his head. "All I know is that an old beggar came to the gates and whispered to the guard. The guard took him to your grandfather, and they talked together like good friends. It was very odd. Why would a fine gentleman like your grandfather be interested in a raggedy old beggar?"

At first Pierre could think of no reason at all. Then he had an inspiration. "A messenger in disguise perhaps."

"But he looked as if he didn't have any sense," Claude said. "Anyway, I didn't see the beggar again." He pointed to the crowded wharf. "What's going on there? What is everybody doing?"

Pierre laughed. "It's always like that when a ship comes in. They're unloading one of Father's ships."

Two lines of men trotted up and down the gangplank. Those coming off the ship bent almost double from the loads on their backs. Some put their bundles on the growing piles on the dock. Others disappeared through doorways of the three- and four-story buildings nearby.

Casks and bales of goods lined the wharf. Merchants examined one after another. Bankers sat behind little booths exchanging money or rendering accounts. A few women in shawls and tiny bonnets picked their way across the slippery cobblestones.

Claude lingered, staring at the scene.

'Hurry, Claude. We must find Father." Pierre almost had to pull the peasant boy through a narrow doorway.

At a small desk in the low-ceilinged room, a clerk was furiously checking off items on a long list.

"Yes, yes, what is it?" he asked, looking up.

"Is my father here?" Pierre asked.

"Oh, excuse me. Yes. He's in the cellar. Go on down."

The boys went down a narrow stairway.

"Who's there?" His father sounded alarmed.

"It's Pierre."

"Oh." Father appeared around a bend of the tunnellike cellar and brushed his hands. Pierre stared at them. Father looked as if he had been digging.

"What is it, son?"

"Grand-père is here on horseback."

Father spoke politely, but he seemed nervous. "I'll come home as soon as I can. Go straight home, both of you. It isn't good to be out on the streets like this in these times."

Outside, Pierre considered Father's words. Of course he would obey, but he could see nothing dangerous so far. It would not be much farther to go home by way of the town square, and Claude could see the shops.

"This way," he said, leading Claude toward a narrow, cobbled street flanked on both sides by jutting apartments.

Claude craned his neck. "Do people live up there?"

Pierre glimpsed a movement at an open window. He pulled Claude back against the wall just as a housewife flung the contents of a slop pail into the street.

Pierre cupped his hands over his mouth and shouted up to her. "Please be careful, madame. You almost wet us through."

A trill of laughter answered him. "Then stay off the streets, you young Huguenots. You have no right to walk them now."

Pierre stopped in astonishment, his mouth open. Was the woman out of her mind? He had never heard such talk from the townspeople before. He stared upward. A young woman stood at the lattice window tucking a strand of hair under her close-fitting cap. Pierre knew her by sight. He had seen her at the port other times when she waited for her husband.

As soon as she saw the boys looking up at her, the young woman began to finger a large cross hanging around her neck and over her wide, shawllike collar.

"How do you know we're Huguenots?" Pierre asked.

"Oh, don't look so blank, you innocents. Look about you. Do you see anyone else on the street?"

It was true. No one else was in sight. Shop doors were latched tight. Along the street other windows opened one by one. Neighbor women leaned their elbows on the windowsills and listened.

"Do you hear the chanting?" the young woman asked. "They'll be here soon." She stamped her foot. "Be off with you both. How dare you desecrate this ground!"

In a daze Pierre tugged at Claude's sleeve. The boys hurried on. A coldness enveloped Pierre, a coldness that had nothing to do with the shadowed, twisting street. He felt frightened and humiliated. Something had changed since the church bells had rung yesterday. It was as if this woman and others watching in silence were waiting for something bad to happen.

A splatter of water nearby made both boys jump. One of the neighbor women had emptied her slop jar in the street. Pierre began to run, with Claude right behind him. One by one the women opened their windows and threw water at the boys. Pierre turned toward the town square. The mocking voices of the housewives followed them.

When the boys reached the sunlit square, Pierre fanned himself a moment with his hat. Claude showed no sign of fatigue.

"Is this the way they treat you all the time?" he asked.

"No. It was never like this before yesterday." Pierre told about the church bells, but did not mention the midnight meeting.

Claude took off his wet jacket and let it dry in the sun. "I don't think I'd like to live in town," he said.

Pierre laughed in a rueful tone. "I didn't know it would be like this, or I wouldn't have brought you this way." He realized he should have obeyed his father.

The boys started across the square just as a church procession emerged from a side street. Men in long gowns with embroidered stoles and cornered hats swayed in time to their chanting. They looked neither to the right nor to the left as they held aloft images and relics on satin pillows.

"Quick! In here, Claude." Pierre motioned to a doorway. "Don't move. Let's hope they don't see us."

But someone had seen them. A man in church robes strode up and seized Pierre by the scruff of the neck. "What do you mean—insulting God? Take off your hat, boy."

Fear tightened Pierre's throat, but he managed to gasp out two words, "I cannot."

"Take your hat off in the presence of God, I say." The man's grip tightened. He shook Pierre, jerking him off his feet.

"But God isn't on that pillow." Pierre was gasping for breath now.

"Why! You young heretic, you!"

Claude gave a mighty push and shoved the priest off balance. "Run, Pierre."

They bolted toward the other end of the square. Claude ran easily. Spurred by fear, Pierre kept up with him. The boys did not stop until they reached the garden gate. Othalie, the maid, opened it at once when Pierre rang.

"What took you so long? I was waiting for you." She led the way to the house.

"What shall we tell the boys?" Mother asked as Pierre and Claude came into the room. She looked as if she had been crying.

"We'll wait until Father comes."

Even after Father came there was no mention of what had happened. It was only after supper, when the family sat around the fire, that Pierre ventured to ask.

Grand-père settled back in his chair. "A long time ago a good king of France promised the Huguenots freedom of worship. We could hold public office and be educated just like anyone else in France. Before that, the Huguenots suffered a great deal because of their beliefs. Their homes were burned, their places of worship torn down. Many lost their lives. But the good king put a stop to that. He was in the town of Nantes at the time, and his written promise was called the Edict of Nantes. About five years ago certain people persuaded the present king to be stricter with the Huguenots. They said we were heretics, that we did not love God. The king listened to these people, and now he has broken the promise made so very long ago. The Edict of Nantes has been revoked."

Pierre guessed at the meaning of the word *revoked*, but he was glad when Claude asked, "What does *revoked* mean?"

"It means the law has been called back. After 87 years of being enforced, it does not exist anymore, as of October 18, 1685. The king will do everything to make us give up our religion."

As he spoke there was a sound of voices outside the garden wall. A stone shattered the window above the window seat and bounced to the floor. A splinter of glass struck Henri on the forehead, and he turned an inquiring gaze to his mother. A trickle of blood flowed from the cut on his head.

The little group sat in stunned silence, as angry voices filled the air.

"The Huguenots are heretics! Kill them! They mock God. Kill them all!"

CHAPTER 3

Threat to freedom

Othalie, the Le Bruns' cook, rocked back and forth, her hands to her face. "Oh, what shall we do?"

Mother was the first to move. She spoke in a low, quick voice. "Othalie, bring water and a cloth to sponge off Henri's forehead."

Father sprang to his feet. "We must load the guns."

"Just a moment, Paul." Grand-père raised both hands as if pushing the idea away. "Those people are still outside the wall. As long as they don't try to break through, there is no need for action."

Father looked astonished. "This from you—a former soldier in the king's army?"

"Don't underestimate me," Grand-père said. "I'm still a good fighter, but only when necessary."

Father walked the length of the long room, pounding a fist into his open palm. "But are we to let them come in and massacre us? Another St. Bartholomew's?"

"No, Paul," Grand-père said. "We shall fight if necessary, but it is not yet the right time to act. I'm sure the mob out there is not organized for an attack. The garden wall is as strong as stone can make it. No one can get through the gate unless the lock is broken."

The voices outside grew fainter.

"You see, they're going away already. They were just a bunch of unorganized hotheads."

Othalie hurried in from the kitchen, carrying a basin of water and soft linen cloths. Henri did not whimper when his mother dabbed at the cut on his forehead.

All was quiet outside. The cold night air pushed through the broken window. Everyone huddled close to the fireplace.

"Grand-père, are all the Catholics going to fight us?" Pierre asked.

"I wouldn't put it that way," Grand-pere said. "I have some good Catholic friends I think we can count on."

"Then who's against us?"

"The Catholics." Grand-père smiled a little. "Excuse me, Pierre; I don't mean to tease you. I'll try to explain. You're a person, aren't you? A single individual? A complete person?"

"Yes, of course, Grand-père."

"And your mother is a person too, isn't she?"

"Why, yes. Everybody's a person."

Grand-père went on. "Catholics are persons too. They have families just as we do—mothers, fathers, children. They eat, sleep, and work, just as we do. Do you understand this, Pierre?"

"Yes."

"And you too, Claude?"

Claude nodded. Pierre wished Grand-père would hurry and explain.

"When it comes to worshipping God, Catholics believe their church is the only one. They want everyone to believe as they do. Some of them honestly believe that the soul of anyone who is not a Catholic will be damned. They call us Huguenots heretics, and they think anything they can do to make us Catholics is better than to let us die without having our souls saved their way."

Pierre looked at Henri. "Then that's why Henri can't go out. The Catholics want to save his soul. I thought they just wanted him."

"Yes, and we Huguenots believe that we can worship God directly by studying the Bible. We don't need priests to speak to God for us. We can pray to God ourselves. We have leaders, yes, like Pastor Foudray, to help us; but the pastor does not stand between us and God. We can talk directly to God. Catholics believe that only priests can talk to God."

There was silence in the room as everyone thought about what Grand-père was saying.

"Henri," he said a moment later, "God will help to keep you safe. You must help Him, though."

"How?" Henri's eyes widened.

"Never speak to strangers or do anything they ask you."

"I won't, Grand-père."

Pierre had more questions to ask. "Are there more Catholics in France than Huguenots?"

"Yes. The Catholics are numbered in the millions."

"But how did the Huguenots dare to fight so many religious wars?"

"Because God was with us," Grand-père said.

Pierre felt a warm exultation, a growing pride that he belonged to such brave believers. "How many wars have we fought?"

"Nine," Grand-père said.

Father broke in. "But this time I think many thousands will leave France."

Pierre did not dare admit he had heard the men talking at the midnight meeting, when they had talked about going to England or the West Indies or America.

"Where can they go?" he asked, wondering whether America would be mentioned again, and whether Othalie would exclaim as she did during the meeting.

"England, Holland, America—" Father said.

Othalie burst into a louder wail than she had made the night before.

"Don't speak of—of America." Her voice quavered. "It's worse than the West Indies. Do you know what they do to immigrants?" She lowered her voice. "They treat them like slaves, like cattle. America is a place worse than death. It is worse than the galleys, even."

"Where did you hear such nonsense, Othalie?" Father used the same word Mother had used the night before.

"Alec said so."

"What does he know about America?"

"He hears a lot of talk at the bakery shop. Everybody comes there at least once a week." Othalie lifted her head with a proud air. Alec was the baker, and Othalie planned to marry him.

"But Othalie, he's Catholic. He's prejudiced."

"Monsieur, once we're married, he'll be a Huguenot. I just know it. He'll do anything for me."

Pierre persisted in his questions. "Can't we get all the Huguenots in France and make a great big army and march up to the king's palace and—"

"At one time we could have. The Huguenots were the best-trained soldiers in the country," Grand-père said. "They fought for their king whenever he needed them, and they will still do so. But it is against the law now for us to drill troops."

"Mother," Pierre asked, "didn't we often watch the soldiers drill?"

"Yes, but the last time you saw them was five years ago, when you were Henri's age. They haven't been allowed to do it since then."

Mother stirred. Henri had fallen asleep in her arms. She signaled Othalie to take him upstairs. Father banked the fire. Pierre and Claude started toward the hall. A rattling at the gate startled everyone. The clamor continued, and then the secret ring sounded, three long peals.

Mother ran to Father. "Has someone betrayed us?"

"I'll get the guns." Father brought one of the guns and placed it on the ledge of the broken window. He motioned to Grand-père. "I'll go out. Keep me covered."

Grand-père sat on the window seat and held the gun.

Mother, white-faced, clung to Father for a moment. Again the three long peals sounded. Father pulled away and went outside. In a moment he came back, followed by Alec Calvet, the baker.

"Why, Alec!" Mother said with a sigh of relief. "What on earth are you doing out tonight?"

"I must see Othalie, Madame Le Brun. Please. I beg you. It is of utmost importance."

"Why, of course, Alec." Mother was as polite as if late-night callers were usual. "I'll call her."

When Othalie came down, Alec, red-faced, took her hands in his. "Father Revrony will call on you tomorrow."

Othalie trembled. "Why does he want to see me?"

"Now, Othalie, we've known this had to be done before we get married. Don't antagonize him. Everything depends on it, especially now . . .

Othalie nodded.

"I can't stay," Alec said. "I just thought you'd better be warned. No one knows what will happen, with the king coming through tomorrow."

"The king!" the whole family exclaimed.

"Yes. We just heard the news. I must go—it's the second rising for my bread dough." Alec babbled a few words of farewell and backed out into the night.

Mother put both hands on Othalie's shoulders. "How did Alec come to know the secret signal?"

Othalie burst into tears. "Madame, I told him. He will be one of the family, and I told him to use it only if there was trouble."

"But can we be sure he won't tell?"

Before Othalie could answer, the gate bell sounded three peals.

"Madame, he wouldn't tell anyone else. I know he wouldn't."

This time Father brought in Pastor Foudray. The pastor was so agitated that he could not speak at first.

"Fifteen days."

These were the first words Pierre understood.

"Fifteen days. Do you understand?"

Mother led him to a chair, and Pastor Foudray clutched the back of it until his knuckles whitened. "My family and I must leave La Rochelle in 15 days. Banished from France. Exiled—to be strangers in a strange land. I don't know where to turn, what to do. We can take only what we can carry on our backs or in a handcart.

Monsieur Le Brun, do you think it is possible for us to hide in the cargo of one of your ships and go to England, or America, or any place at all?"

Father took a deep breath. "Not only that, Pastor. We can store supplies in my cellar at the port. I have told no one this—not even my wife—but I have been secretly excavating down there for the past four years, a handful of dirt at a time, so no one would suspect."

Pastor Foudray's face became so radiant that Pierre felt tears start. Why would anyone want to make a kind man like Pastor Foudray leave his country?

"So many of our people have already fled," the pastor said. "I used to wonder how they managed. Now I know that there is always a way out." He left with a smile.

Early the next morning the household was astir. Father left for the port, and Grand-père and Claude started on their return journey to the estate. Othalie kept dropping spoons and kettles, jumping at every sound. It was almost a relief when the priest, Father Revrony, came. But to Pierre's horror, the priest turned out to be the same man who had ordered him to remove his hat when the church procession passed. Had he recognized Pierre?

The priest glanced around the room. "May I talk to Mademoiselle Othalie in private?"

Mother stiffened. "Othalie is part of the family, Father Revrony. She is one of us."

"It is about the marriage plans and the church, Madame Le Brun." Father Revrony stood unmoving.

Othalie clasped her hands and looked from one to the other. Mother made a gesture of helplessness. "You may talk over there by the window seat, if you wish."

She pushed Pierre and Henri ahead of her down the narrow passageway through the kitchen. Pierre was consumed with curiosity. What would the priest say to Othalie? As soon as the boys were outside, Pierre cried, "Let's play follow the leader." Without waiting for Henri's reply, Pierre dropped on his hands and knees and began to crawl near the shrubbery. Henri followed.

At the side of the house Pierre put his fingers to his lips. "Now we're going to play that we're being hunted by Catholics. If you make even the slightest sound, you'll be taken prisoner and sent to a convent school."

Henri dropped like a stone, and Pierre crawled ahead. Under the window he rose up and peeped inside. Othalie sat on the window seat, with head down and her hands in her lap. Father Revrony faced the window.

"You understand that your children must be raised in the

church." Father Revrony gazed at Othalie with unblinking eyes.

Pierre could hear every word. "I can't agree to that."

"Don't you realize, my poor ignorant child, that the souls of your children will be forever lost unless they are baptized as Catholics?"

From the movement of Othalie's arm, Pierre guessed she was wiping her eyes.

'But I am a Huguenot. I have worked for the Le Bruns since I was 12. They are the kindest people I have ever known."

Father Revrony nodded. "I quite agree that they may be kind. They are hardworking and wealthy, too. But their souls are damned to eternal torment for their heretical beliefs, and so will yours be too—and anybody else's, even if that someone were in my own family." The priest's voice shook with emotion. He paused, as if he had gotten off the subject. "God asks me to bring Him souls, and I must win them." He stabbed his forefinger at Othalie. "Will you crucify our Lord by casting the souls of your unborn children into the lake of fire and brimstone for eternity?"

Pierre, in terror and fascination at the priest's tirade, had forgotten to crouch below the window level. He inched upward to get a clearer view of the priest and gradually straightened up, held spellbound by the priest's words and tone.

Father Revrony's voice thundered on. "Will you deliberately be a murderer of children's souls?" He stepped forward, towering over Othalie.

Pierre must have made some movement, for he found himself staring into the eyes of Father Revrony, who took still another step forward. The priest's mouth went slack with surprise. Priest and boy gazed at each other. The look of fury on the man's face turned into an expression of cruel calculation.

Something nudged Pierre's leg. He looked down. Henri had

crawled on all fours to the window. The priest looked down at Henri and frowned. Slowly his mouth twitched into a one-sided smile. In panic, Pierre seized Henri's hand and ran.

CHAPTER 4

Unfriendly Visitors

Pierre pulled Henri behind the bushes and to the mud fort. Henri clung to Pierre's hand. "Is that man going to take me away?"

"Not if he doesn't see you." Pierre's voice was grim. "Look! There he goes."

Father Revrony strode with long, quick steps to the gate. He glanced around the garden before opening the latch. The gate slammed shut behind him.

Pierre stood up and stretched his cramped legs. "He can't get back in now."

A muffled, steady beat sounded from a distance.

"It's drums," Pierre said. "The king is coming."

The boys jumped in excitement, just as the garden gate bell rang three steady peals. Pierre ran to open the gate. He gasped at the sight of Claude standing outside with torn and muddy clothes, scratched face, and dirt-streaked hair. His horse looked winded.

"Hide me, Pierre. They're after me."

Mother and Othalie ran out from the house. Othalie began to moan.

"Mercy on us! They've murdered this poor boy."

"It's Claude," Pierre said.

"Whatever happened?" Mother asked as she put her arms around Claude and helped him to the house.

Claude panted out his story. "We were on the way to Grand-père's estate, and we met the dragoons. They all passed by except for the last few. One of them asked if we were Catholics or Huguenots, and of course monsieur told the truth. They said, 'La Lanterne prison is where we keep Huguenots now.' One of the dragoons shot off a musket, and it frightened our horses. Monsieur's horse went one way and mine the other. He got away, because I saw him go into the woods. There are hundreds of hiding places there. I know. I used to hide from the hunters."

Claude let Othalie sponge off his face.

"I hid in the field for a while and then came here."

Shouts rose outside the garden wall. "Open in the name of the king!"

Othalie shrieked and bit her fist. "They'll kill us all!"

Claude cried in alarm, "Where can I hide?"

The thunderous command came again. "Open at once, or we'll fire!"

"The window seat!" Henri said, jumping in excitement. "Hide him in the window seat."

For a second Mother looked blank. "Yes, yes. That's it. Hurry."

The boys ran to the front room. Pierre flung back the lid, and Claude climbed in. The dragoons poured into the yard.

"We're looking for a peasant boy who got away. He's here. His horse is outside. Turn him over to us."

Mother spoke in a calm voice. "You are welcome to search the house if you think he is here."

The dragoons tramped from room to room. Before they started upstairs, one of them stopped the others. "We can't waste time like this. The boy isn't downstairs. We have to be at the square by the time the duke's carriage arrives. There's plenty of time for this sort of thing afterward."

The dragoons thumped their short muskets on the floor as they left.

Claude laughed in relief as he stepped out of his hiding place.

"That's over." Mother smiled and nodded her head in satisfaction. "I've thought of a plan. We'll disguise you, Claude, and you can come with us to see the king. Pierre, bring him a suit of your clothes. No one will know he's the same boy."

Pierre brought out a hip-length doublet with turned-down collar and cuffs of lace, and leather shoes with large rosettes. Claude put on his new clothes, stepping gingerly into the shoes. Mother and Othalie put on bonnets, outdoor capes, and gloves.

With ears and eyes alert, Pierre led the way.

"We must hurry," Mother said. "Father will be waiting at the port. Othalie, bring the key to the garden gate, or we'll lock ourselves out."

"Yes, madame. I have it around my neck. Oh, madame, imagine—the king himself is coming. He'll put an end to all this trouble, I'm sure."

They hurried along the seawall. Pierre pointed to a tower standing high and threatening above two forts.

"There's the prison, Claude. That's La Lanterne."

Othalie twitched her shawl close. "I wonder how many of our people are already in prison there."

Henri stared. "Is that where they'd take me?"

"No. They wouldn't put children there," Mother said.

Pierre, walking ahead with Claude, waited until Mother caught up. "Tell Claude about the women pouring boiling pitch, Mother." Pierre never tired of hearing about the siege of La Rochelle in 1627, when Grand-père was Pierre's age.

Without slowing her steps, Mother pointed to the remains of an ancient wall. "A long time ago these walls closed in the whole town. Soldiers tried to capture La Rochelle, but the people locked the gates and wouldn't come out."

"And then what?" Henri excitedly tugged at his mother's hand.

"The women helped defend the city. They boiled pitch in a huge caldron, got it up on the wall somehow, and poured it onto the soldiers."

"Did the children help too?" Henri asked.

"Yes, they helped. Grand-père was there, and he remembers."

"But the soldiers captured La Rochelle, didn't they?" Pierre asked, although he knew the answer already.

"Yes, but not for months and months—more than a year, in fact. The people did not give up until the food ran out."

"Mother, if we ever had to escape, we could go to the island of Rè or Oleron. Rè would be safer. There's no fort there." Pierre pointed to the island nearly opposite La Rochelle. The area between was a low, sandy marshland. "Father could anchor one of his ships there, and we could go out in small boats. We'd lie flat, and no one would see us."

"Hush. Don't talk like that." Othalie gave Pierre a little push. "Nobody is going to have to escape from La Rochelle. This is where we've always lived."

Pierre and Claude ran ahead to find Father and tell him what had happened. Flags and banners fluttered from every window on the streets leading to the square. People leaned out, laughing and talking, while they waited for the army to enter. People jostled one another in the streets as well, trying to find the best place to see.

The drumbeats grew louder. Trumpets played stirring tunes.

"I've never seen the king," Claude said. Pierre had to admit he had not seen him either.

"Here they come!"

Four trumpeters marched first, then the musketeers. After them the pikemen held their steel-pointed wooden shafts high. They were all dressed in bright colors. Everyone wore a ruff, a plumed hat, and yellow, red, or striped doublets. The provost guard had on a scarlet coat with gold frogs. Musicians wore gold and silver lace at their throats and wrists. The cavalrymen and dragoons were most colorful of all in their red breeches, high black boots, and blue coats.

The soldiers marched in formation, almost filling the square. They turned and stood at attention, facing the entrance. A carriage gleaming with gold-painted carvings rumbled over the cobblestones.

A hush fell over the townspeople. A guard opened the carriage door.

There was a gasp of dismay from every throat. This was not the king.

"Who is it?" The question flew from person to person. "It's the Duke de Guichot."

"Why is he here and not the king?"

"We must wait and see."

The duke, a tall man with a hooked nose and thin lips, mounted a horse and unrolled a scroll. He waited until the last rustle of the crowd had died away, and then he began to read in a resounding voice. Even then Pierre could catch only a few words at a time.

"The king has authorized me to read this message to his subjects. . . . The original purpose of the Edict of Nantes was to win over heretics. . . . This object is now accomplished, inasmuch as our subjects of the pretended Reformed religion have embraced the true faith."

The crowd murmured. The duke stiffly waited for silence.

"The Edict of Nantes remains therefore superfluous. It is no longer in effect."

A sound like the tide rippled through the crowd.

"If there be any Reformed pastors among you, they must leave the kingdom within 15 days." The duke stared over the heads of the crowd. "But if they should reform and join the one true religion, they will receive a third more salary."

There was an indignant undertone, quickly subdued. Pierre saw Pastor Foudray edge up to his parents and whisper something.

"In broad daylight?" Pierre heard Mother say.

"It's best now before the dragoons are quartered in our homes."

Mother and Father nodded.

"If any Huguenots have already fled the kingdom," the duke went on, they are to return within four months, or all their property will be taken."

No one stirred.

"Parents are hereby forbidden to instruct children in the Reformed religion. Every child in the kingdom is to be baptized as a Catholic."

This time there was an outcry, a piercing scream from Othalie, who turned and held Henri tight.

"Othalie! Control yourself." Mother's voice was icy. "You will get us all into trouble."

The duke spoke to one of his aides in a loud, contemptuous tone. "I believe that at the end of the month there won't be a Huguenot left in La Rochelle."

A buzz of conversation rose. This time the duke made no attempt to stem the chatter.

Mother bent down and spoke to Pierre and Claude in a whisper. "We are going to slip through the crowd little by little and go to the meetinghouse. Move slowly so that no one notices, and always face the duke. Do you understand?"

The boys nodded. The duke started to talk again.

"It is illegal as of today for any household to have a Bible. There will be no meetings of any kind other than those in the Catholic church."

Pierre and Claude started to make their way to the edge of the crowd. An aide said something to the duke, who straightened and called out in a loud voice, "No one of the Reformed religion will be permitted to marry a Catholic."

Pierre heard Othalie gasp.

"If any Catholic should turn to the Reformed religion, his property will be confiscated, and he will be banished from the kingdom. The same will happen to anyone who harbors a Huguenot refugee."

Pierre braced himself for another outcry from Othalie, but he heard nothing except a muffled sob.

The duke was beginning to sound hoarse. "But if a Huguenot becomes a Catholic, all his debts will be deferred for three years. He will be exempt from taxation for two years. No dragoons will be quartered in his home."

The word *dragonnade* passed from one person to another. To Pierre it sounded like another word for death. The duke must have heard. His thin lips twitched in a sneer. "I see you all know what the dragonnade is."

Mother paled as she heard the word, and Pierre knew why. A dragonnade meant dragoons would live with them. Grand-père had spoken of dragoons coming and living with people without paying for food or lodging.

Pierre, Claude, and the rest of the family were at the very edge of the square by this time. Pierre saw the duke motion to an aide, who handed him a big black book.

"The king takes his authority from the Bible, Luke 14, verse 23: 'And the lord said unto the servant, Go out into the highways and hedges, and compel them to come in, that my house may be filled.' Citizens of La Rochelle, we are the servants of God . . .'"

Pierre did not listen to any more. He saw his parents and Othalie and Henri slip into an alleyway. Pierre and Claude hurried to catch up with them.

They almost ran to the Huguenot meetingplace, entering under the main archway, with its finely sculptured stone displaying the arms of the kings of France and Navarre. A number of Huguenot businessmen and their families were already inside, waiting in silence on the plain benches. Pastor Foudray and his family sat near the front.

"This may be the last time we shall ever meet like this," Mother said in a whisper. "Try to remember the service."

Pierre showed Claude the raised seats reserved for magistrates and other dignitaries of the city. Behind the seats a tablet hung on the wall. The Ten Commandments were inscribed in letters of gold on a blue background.

The service started in the usual way. The reader read from the Bible, and the congregation rose when Pastor Foudray made the invocation and prayer.

"We will join in Luther's hymn, 'Strong Tower and Refuge Is Our God,'" the pastor said. The singing was subdued yet intense. Pierre, like other Huguenots, loved to sing.

Pastor Foudray's voice trembled as he began the sermon. "God has fed and clothed us, and even granted us considerable estates, after this promise of Christ in the nineteenth chapter of

Matthew: 'Every one that hath forsaken houses, or brethren, or sisters, or father, or mother, or wife, or children, or lands, for my name's sake, shall receive an hundredfold, and shall inherit everlasting life.' Now the time has come, my brethren, when we must forsake our houses and lands."

A clatter outside the meetinghouse stopped him for a few seconds. The congregation stirred.

Pastor Foudray talked in a firm voice, but his words came faster, as if he were racing against time. "We shall put on the whole armor of God. 'We wrestle not against flesh and blood, but against . . . powers, against the rulers of the darkness of this world.'"

Shouts sounded. "Destroy it! Tear it down!"

The pastor raised his voice. "We must not fail the task before us. We must arm ourselves with truth."

The shouts outside intensified.

Pastor Foudray did not falter. He clenched the sides of the pulpit until his knuckles showed white. "Put on the 'breastplate of righteousness; . . . taking the shield of faith,' 'the helmet of salvation, and the sword of the Spirit.'"

Thunder sounded at the door, a trampling and a pounding that drowned out the rest of Pastor Foudray's words. With a mighty crash the door swung hack. A group of pikemen held their weapons straight ahead of them. Pierre had never seen anything so cruel-looking as the long wooden shafts with their pointed steel tips.

CHAPTER 5

Conversion by force

The pikemen crouched over their weapons as if they expected the Huguenots to fight, and they moved into the church with relentless force.

Pastor Foudray stood behind his pulpit in quiet dignity. A pikeman motioned to him to step down, but the pastor did not move. The pikeman drew his wooden shaft back in a threatening gesture, but a disturbance at the back of the building made him pause. A captain pushed his way to the front and turned to the congregation. He drew his sword halfway out of its sheath, but the absolute silence on the part of the Huguenots seemed to wilt his fierceness. He scowled and began to pace up and down.

"This is a den of iniquity," he began, and turned to glare at the pastor. At that moment a ray of sunlight struck the gold letters of the Ten Commandments hanging on the wall. The captain choked, lowered his eyes, and threw back his shoulders. Then he began to shout.

"This house of desecration must be destroyed until not one sign of it remains. Stone by stone, with your own hands, you will remove this work of the devil."

The captain motioned to his men. "If there is anything here you would like, go ahead and take it. Otherwise, we'll burn everything."

The soldiers began to strip the room. One man jabbed his

pike into the tablet with the Ten Commandments, and then cut the cord that held the tablet to the wall. Two of his companions carried it outside. Others wrenched the pulpit from its place, staggering under the weight. The pastor's Bible fell to the floor. A pikeman plunged his pike through it and bore it out ahead of him, as if the Bible were something loathsome.

"Everybody outside." The captain emphasized his command with a wave of his sword. No one moved.

"No one will be hurt if you obey. We promise safety."

The soldiers herded the congregation into the front yard, where a fire was already blazing. The men threw the pulpit, the tablet, the Bible, and the congregation's hymnbooks into the blaze. Soldiers ran in and out of the building, bringing papers and ledgers.

"The church certificates!" Dr. Maurice, the Huguenot historian, wrung his hands.

Pastor Foudray looked dazed as he watched the papers burn. "Those are our baptismal records. They can never be duplicated."

For a long time the only sounds were the crackle of flames and the exclamations of the soldiers. Pierre watched in horrified silence.

A group of city officials hurried through the archway, the mayor in the lead, puffing from his exertion.

The captain greeted him. "The way is now open for the extermination of the Huguenots, if necessary."

The mayor fingered the lace at his throat nervously.

"Why have these heretics been allowed to worship so long?" the captain asked.

The mayor was apologetic. "Under the edict, you know, they had the right."

"The edict is revoked. If they try to worship now, we'll use the sword."

"The Huguenots have brought a lot of business to La Rochelle," the mayor said, with a timid glance at the congregation. "Conversion by force will make hypocrites, not believers, will it not?"

The captain ignored the first remark. "We'll have believers. Don't you know that the king has said, 'To bring back all my subjects to Catholic unity, I would readily, with one hand, cut off the other'?"

Dr. Maurice stepped up to the two men. His regal bearing, as of a man used to authority, checked the captain's gesture of impatience. "The Huguenots have been loyal to the king. Their loyalty has been unquestioned. They are good soldiers, too."

"Heretics are never loyal." The captain did not speak rudely. "But as for being soldiers, we'll harass the inhabitants of La Rochelle until they consume both their gunpowder and their bullets."

Dr. Maurice continued. "Does not monsieur the captain believe heretics should be led to the church by the hand—not the hair?"

The captain snapped out his reply. "The sword shall lead them."

All the time the officials talked, the Huguenots kept the same silence as before. Pierre saw Father beckon to Pastor Foudray.

"You must leave tonight, Pastor," he said.

"Tonight? How can I? It is impossible. I cannot yield either to consternation or cowardice." The pastor's face worked with emotion.

"Pastor Foudray, at the slightest excuse the dragoons may start murdering and pillaging. You see what it is like already. Do not chance your family's safety."

"But how can we leave?"

"Bring your family to the port tonight," Father said. "Do not bring any belongings, but wear all the clothes you can put on. We do not want anything suspicious to start the dragoons questioning you. I'll hide you in the cellar until the ship is ready to sail."

Pastor Foudray appeared dazed yet attentive. "Tonight? Is it really tonight?"

"Yes, the dragoons will be quartered by evening."

"Ah, yes, the dragonnade. My grandfather spoke of such things long ago." The pastor bowed his head. "If this is the yoke, God's will be done. We'll be there tonight, somehow. Thank you."

Pierre watched the mayor argue with the captain. "He has courage, hasn't he, Father?"

Father answered with a wry smile. "He has good reason to be courageous—he has invested much money in the cargo my ships bring back."

A dragoon came up and saluted the captain. "Shall we start converting?"

The captain nodded.

"Line up against the wall," the dragoons commanded the Huguenots.

The simple command struck terror in Pierre such as he had never felt before. His tongue felt thick, and he panted hard, as though he had been running.

"Are they going to kill us?" Claude whispered.

Pierre tried to answer, but no words came out.

A Huguenot woman called out to the dragoons, "You promised us safety."

The captain answered her in a contemptuous tone. "Faith need not be kept with heretics."

The leader of the dragoons stopped in front of the cobbler's wife, who rocked her baby in her arms.

"I want to see a show of hands from all of you who wish to be converted to Catholicism. Do you?" he asked, addressing the cobbler's wife.

"No, of course not."

The dragoon unsheathed his sword and waved it in front of the baby's face. The mother's eyes widened, and she shrank back, shielding the baby from the sword.

"Are you willing to be a Catholic?" the dragoon asked.

The baby cooed and reached for the gleaming sword.

"No, baby. No, no." The mother turned away.

"Don't you think you could be persuaded?" With his sword the dragoon flicked a few hairs off the baby's head. The baby began to cry. The cobbler's wife sank to her knees, protecting the baby's head with her body.

"Yes—yes. I'll do it. Don't hurt my child." She choked over the words.

"Then you are voluntarily seeking to have your child baptized in the Catholic Church?" The dragoon turned his sword over and over.

The woman's shoulders heaved as she nodded.

"Take her to the church," the leader commanded. Two dragoons escorted the weeping woman through the archway.

The captain had watched the scene with folded arms and a look of haughty contempt. "For my part, I would kill them all. God will know His own." He spoke to the tax collector. "Mark down one conversion and one baptism."

The tax collector opened his record book and made the marks. "Thirty-nine million people in France," he said in a conversational tone. "Six hundred fifty thousand are Protestant. We shall soon convert them all."

The leader of the dragoons walked briskly past the waiting

Huguenots. "Are the rest of you ready to be converted?"

No one replied.

"What are your orders, sir?" the dragoon asked.

With an air of weariness the captain shrugged. "We need women to cook and wash for us. They'd better go home and get busy."

Once again the word *dragonnade* passed through the congregation.

"What does that word mean, Mother?" Henri asked.

"It means soldiers will come and stay at our house."

"A lot of them could stay with us, our house is so big."

"Hush."

The captain surveyed the Huguenots. He stood with feet apart and hands on hips. "The tax collector will assign the best houses for quartering the dragoons."

Afterward the Huguenots moved toward the archway. The dragoons let them by.

"You go on home," Father said to Mother. "I'll arrange to go to the port." He turned to the mayor. "I have some cargo that would interest you, if you would like to come to the port with me. Luxury items from Spain—gold goblets and jewels your wife would be interested in. Under the circumstances, I could let you have them quite cheap." The mayor's face lighted up. "Why, yes, Monsieur Le Brun, I'd like to see them."

Mother, Othalie, and the three boys started home. As they passed the bakery shop, Pierre heard a low call. Alec beckoned from the side door. He loaded three long loaves of bread into Pierre's arms, and three more into Claude's. "If there's any trouble, get word to me." He closed the door without a sound.

Once home, Mother and Othalie began supper preparations. The three boys helped pare and dice a mountain of vegetables.

It seemed only a little while before the command came. "Open in the name of the king." Shouting and singing, the dragoons poured through the gateway. Pierre watched from the corner of the house.

"You don't need a gate," they said, and with grunts and heaves they dislodged the gate and ruined the lock.

"Oh, madame," Othalie said, "it's a whole regiment!" She knelt on the floor with her arms around Henri.

"Stand up, Othalie," Mother said. "We must be calm."

The captain and the tax collector came inside first. Pierre followed them and went to stand with Claude, who had not budged from the kitchen when the dragoons had stormed into the yard.

"A fine large house you have here, Madame—uh—" the captain looked at a name in the record book, "Madame Le Brun. We have you down for 10. How many could you conveniently quarter?"

Mother hesitated. "Ten would be the maximum."

The captain walked through the house and back.

"Ten could sleep right there in the front room. I'll put you down for 20."

Othalie's lips quivered. "But that is impossible."

Her distress left the captain unmoved. "Things are different now. Many impossibilities are going to be quite possible. Go ahead with supper. The men are hungry."

A messenger ran in calling for the captain. "The duke says Huguenots are leaving La Rochelle by the hundreds. No one has seen them go, but their houses are vacant."

The captain strode up and down in a fury. "What fools they are! Don't they know we have orders to kill anyone trying to get away?"

Still fuming, the captain left with the tax collector. The dragoons started coming into the house. One stopped to read the inscription over the front door.

"Une foi, une loi, une roi," he said in a loud voice. "We'll have to drink to that—one faith, one law, one king. We'll make this motto come true."

The dragoons roamed over the house, exclaiming as they pawed over the fine furnishings. One almost fell downstairs carrying a hand-carved cradle with a gabled roof.

"Baby in this house?"

"No," Mother said.

"Good. My wife will like this."

Pierre remembered the chest with the guns. To his relief, it was empty. Father had taken the guns to the port.

One of the dragoons picked up the family Bible and psalter from the mantel. "You won't need these anymore." He burned them in the fireplace.

"What's this?" someone asked, taking down a hank of unspun flax from the wall. "What's it doing up there?"

"It signifies that this house will never lack what future generations need," Mother explained.

Two dragoons were quarreling over the tapestry. One was taking it off the wall and the other grabbed it.

"This is mine. First come, first served," one said.

"Let's shoot dice for it."

"Agreed."

They got down on their hands and knees. Other dragoons came to watch. Two or three tried to run the spinning wheel. Soon the heavy cranks were out of order.

At least they did not stay long in the kitchen. Othalie, with housewifely pride, defied them all.

"If you want something to eat, stay out of here." She stamped her foot. "If you bother me, you'll get no food!"

Pierre had never heard her so angry. To escape her tongue-lashing, the dragoons stumbled over themselves getting out of the kitchen.

Mother kept Henri right by her all the time. Pierre and Claude tried to keep out of the dragoons' way, but they could not resist watching and listening to them.

One of the dragoons found Pierre's schoolbooks. He beckoned to the boys.

"Here, read this to me."

Pierre reached for the book, but the dragoon shoved it in front of Claude, who hung back.

"You read it."

Claude looked at the dragoon, a stricken expression crossing his face. He shook his head.

"I said read this."

"I can't read." Claude tried to smile.

"Can't read? You live in a fine house like this and can't even read? Haven't you gone to school?"

"No."

"I have," Pierre said, hoping it would help.

"Never mind about you. What is your name?" he asked Claude.

"Claude."

"Claude who?"

Claude stammered a reply. "Arnaud."

"Relation of the Le Bruns?"

"No."

The dragoon thumped his musket on the floor. "Say, here's a kid that doesn't even belong to the family," he said in a loud voice. The others quieted.

"A runaway Huguenot, huh?"

Claude squirmed.

"Didn't you hear what we do to runaways?"

"Yes, but—"

Another dragoon called out, "Make a convert of him—that'll be one more for the record."

The dragoon drew out a cross and attached it to the muzzle of his musket.

"Kiss the cross, Claude."

"No."

The dragoon forced Claude step by step back to the wall. Pierre looked on, weak with horror, not knowing what would happen, and powerless to help.

"Kiss the cross."

The musket tip touched Claude's face. He could not move. Pierre turned away sobbing at the unbearable sight.

CHAPTER 6

A Child for the Church

An indignant outcry sounded loudly from the doorway leading to the kitchen. Othalie stood wiping her hands on her apron.

"Supper is ready," she snapped.

The dragoon who was trying to force Claude to kiss the cross did not lower his musket.

Othalie's lips were tight. Her eyes flashed. "It's ready right now."

The men became cheerful at once. They pulled their companion off Claude and propelled the man to the long supper table.

Later Father came home and learned what had happened. He looked at the dragoons sprawled over the house, drinking and playing cards.

"We cannot tolerate this," he said to Mother. "Our lives are at the mercy of their whims. I shall take the boys to Grand-père's tonight."

"But the Foudrays—what about them?"

"They're already on their way to England. I sent them by rowboat to the island of Rè. They'll board one of my ships before daylight."

Mother's lips trembled. "I know God is always with us, but it is hard, just the same." She looked at the boys. "You won't be able to sleep tonight until very late. And Henri—how will he manage?"

"Mother—" Henri looked reproachful. "I can walk." Mother sighed. "So much is happening and so fast. But I agree that it will be better if the boys are at Grand-père's."

"We won't take anything with us," Father said. "That way we won't look like refugees."

Late that night, when the dragoons were in a stupor from drinking, Father sent the boys outside. Pierre heard his quick footsteps coming toward the front door.

A thick, hoarse voice roared, "Stop, Monsieur Le Brun." It was a dragoon, belligerent with drink.

The three boys huddled against the wall and listened.

"Were you going someplace, Monsieur Le Brun?"

"Just out to get a little fresh air," Father said.

"Don't go. I want to talk to you, monsieur, about these Reformed preachers."

"Yes?" Father's impatience alarmed Pierre.

"I say banish them—all of them. Don't you agree?"

Father did not answer.

"Monsieur Le Brun, I expect a civil answer." There was a sound of scuffling.

"Where will you banish them?" Father asked.

"That's better. Now we can carry on a civilized conversation, between gentlemen. What was I saying? Oh, yes, slay them all. God will know His own. That's what our captain said." The dragoon laughed, a long, drawling sound, ending with hiccups.

"Yes, sir, Monsieur Le Brun—hang them all, or shoot them. Burn their houses. Start a blaze a mile wide. Don't you agree?"

Father's words were indistinguishable.

"Monsieur Le Brun, you are tired, I see. It has been a long and memorable day." The dragoon laughed again. "We'll lock the house up for the night. Housekeeper! Fetch the keys! No, monsieur, don't go. You and I will have a little nightcap together after we lock up."

Pierre heard the key turn in the lock. "The back way—hurry," he whispered to the others. The three boys ran to the back door, but it was already locked. Shivering from the cold, Pierre and Claude put Henri between them and huddled close to the door until morning. Othalie found them there when she got up to start breakfast.

"You poor lambs. Thank God you are safe." She brought blankets and bedded the boys near the vegetable storeroom. "I'll tell Father what happened. He's asleep now. The dragoons kept him awake all night. He was afraid you had tried to go on to Grandpère's house alone."

Later when the boys woke up, the house was empty.

"Drill." Othalie bit off the word with a nod of satisfaction. "They all had to go and drill so they'd hit their mark better. But they're out of the house, and that's a relief." She seemed almost in good humor as she prepared breakfast for the boys. "Your mother went with your father to make plans." She dropped her voice to a whisper.

"Maybe you're going to take a boat trip."

Pierre was quick to perceive that she did not include herself. "Aren't you going with us?"

Othalie's gay mask dropped, leaving her face careworn. "No, I shall never leave here. Never."

"Where will we go?" Henri asked.

"To some other country—some place that wants you and will treat you as if you belonged."

Claude listened with an anxious expression. "I must go back to your grand-père's estate," he said. "That is where I belong. I'd better go right now."

"In the daylight?" Pierre asked.

"Yes. I know how to hide; don't worry about me. But these clothes—" He looked down at the fine suit the Le Bruns had given him. "Othalie, may I have my own clothes back?"

"Why, they're filthy and torn. You poor child, you don't want those. I should have burned them up."

But Claude was determined to change.

"Keep the shoes, Claude. They'll protect your feet," Pierre said, but Claude refused to wear them.

"I feel better without them. I'd better go while the streets are empty, and I'm not going to try to find my horse. I'll walk."

"Wait! Take some bread and cheese." Othalie cut off a thick slice of bread and a slab of cheese. Claude tucked them in his shirt, and with a quick look outside, he darted through the gate.

A moment later Mother ran into the house. "I just met Claude. He was so determined to go that I didn't have the heart to say no. He's sure your grand-père is home by this time."

Mother examined the boys for any sign of illness after their night outdoors, and then told them the news.

"They say that hundreds are going to Holland, and that already La Lanterne has 100 prisoners. The streets are piled with furniture offered for sale, but if anyone buys goods from 'heretics'" —she isolated the word—"they will be fined and imprisoned."

A man's voice interrupted her. "Anybody home?" Othalie groaned.

It was the tax collector. He came right in without waiting, his mouth turned up in a bland smile. His eyelids fluttered as if he could not bear the light of day. He held the dreaded record book open in his hand.

"The salt tax is payable," he said. "Six times seven is forty-two. That will be twenty-seven francs."

Mother said, "But there are only five in the family."

"The guest you have had with you is the sixth." The tax collector's smile widened. "I have been informed you have bought other salt at the warehouse. Do you have your certificate?"

Mother produced the signed form and paid the tax.

"You plan to be here for some time, do you not?" the tax collector asked, looking about.

"Why, yes. This is our home. Is there any reason we should leave it?" Two bright spots appeared on Mother's cheeks.

"No, of course not. But if you should ever think of leaving—in a hurry, perhaps, as some of your friends have left—there are two big chests I wouldn't be ashamed of having in my own home."

Othalie began to sputter, but Mother remained calm. "I am flattered that you find our furniture worthy of your consideration."

The tax collector did not seem to notice the tone of irony in Mother's voice. He snapped his record book shut and started out of the house.

"Ah," Pierre heard him exclaim. A whining voice responded.

"Madame Le Brun," the tax collector said from the doorway, "you have a visitor." He left with an air of disdain.

A shabbily dressed man shuffled inside. His hair and beard were dusty, his hand-me-down coat had no buttons. A flap pocket hung loose. His shoes were in shreds.

"May I serve you?" Mother asked, as she always did to those who came to beg.

The beggar looked up with eyes of astonishing brightness. He closed them and stood with his head bowed. Pierre was reminded of something. Where had he heard about a beggar recently? Then he remembered. Claude had said that a beggar had come to Grand-père's. Was this the same man, and was he a messenger in disguise?

Pierre looked at the man with new interest, trying to detect some sign of another identity, but he saw nothing unusual. The man's beard and hair were matted, as well as dirty. From the musty odor of his clothes, he had not taken them off for weeks.

"Madame Le Brun?"

'Why, yes. How did you know my name?"

"I have a message for you." The beggar fumbled through his clothes and drew out a sheet of paper folded several times. Mother opened it.

"Why, it's blank. What does this mean?"

The beggar's disconcerting gaze swept over them. "Wet it. But wait until I am gone." He began a whining chant. "Bread, for the love of God, bread."

There was something authoritative about his manner. Othalie brought bread without a word. As soon as the beggar left, Mother got a cup of water. She held the paper to the light. It looked untouched. She dipped it into the water.

"I can see writing," she said, holding it up. "It says, 'Send the boys at once.' How strange! Your grand-père has never done anything like this before. Look."

She showed the others an odd-looking word as signature. Pierre sounded it out.

"*Eidgenossen*. What does it mean?"

"It's the word they use in Switzerland—people like us. Your grand-père always claimed that that was where the Huguenots came from. It means confederate, or oath fellow. I remember he used to say the word *Huguenot* was *Eidgenossen* mispronounced."

"Mother, what do you think the danger is?" Pierre asked.

"What more could there be?"

"Whatever it is, we'll have to tell Father at once. Pierre, do you think you could slip down to the port and find him? Othalie and I will stay here with Henri. The dragoons will be coming back soon, so hurry."

At the port Pierre kept out of sight by moving close to the casks lined up on the wharf. When he found Father and explained the message, Father sighed. Then his expression turned to one of complete astonishment.

"Pastor Foudray! What are you doing here?"

Pierre whirled around. The pastor was just entering the office, his finger to his lips.

"Take me to the cellar. I'll explain there."

Pierre followed the men to the cold underground room.

"It's all right, Brother Le Brun. I brought my family back for the time remaining. I could not leave France yet. It is not in this way that God wills my deliverance. I have a mission to perform. It's all because of a beggar I met last night. He didn't even beg. He just asked me whether I knew that 300 Huguenot families had become 'new converts' of Rome. I couldn't forget his words."

Pastor Foudray held his hand above the candle that Father had lighted.

"Am I to extinguish the light that has been given me, as if I were snuffing out a candle? No. Before I go, something can be done for those who want to emigrate. Inspiration has simply flooded me. We can organize our people—meet in the woods, the hills, help them disguise themselves and evade the guards that are posted everywhere."

"I'll help," Father said.

"Tell him about our beggar, Father."

Pastor Foudray was puzzled at the incident. "He's like a master spy. How does he know so much?"

Father and Pierre went outside. Pierre was pleased to see the respect that bankers and merchants showed his father.

"The richest man in the port," someone said. "His trading ships bring him a fortune every month."

"And honest, too," another added. "His word is his bond. Even if he isn't a Catholic, I'd rather do business with him than anyone else."

"But it's too bad he can't be converted," a third said.

Pierre thought about conversion when Father Revrony and two other priests appeared at the house after supper. They searched the house for Bibles and hymnbooks. When they entered the kitchen, Othalie lost all her bravado. She backed away with a frightened look.

Father Revrony smiled at Henri. "When is this fine young boy going to be converted?"

No one answered.

"I do not believe in conversion by force," the priest said. "God accepts only inclination and free choice."

He stooped to speak to Henri. "Do you want to burn in hell-fire, my son?"

Henri shrank back. "No."

Father Revrony nodded to the other two priests. They lifted Henri up. Each took an arm.

"You see? He has stated in the presence of witnesses that he is not a heretic. He is of age, and he has chosen to become a Catholic. His soul will be saved."

In an aside he spoke to the other priests. His voice was charged with emotion. "Ah, if God would only inspire my own brother to save his soul. To think that a child I don't even know has cried out for the truth." He appeared to be shaken with feelings not related to the present.

"Father," one of the priests said, "we know your trials. Do not give up hope. Your brother may still return to the church."

Father Revrony raised his hand as if to bless the family. His voice was smooth and stern. "If I were you, I would make no outcry. It is deplorable, but the dragoons have been drinking. Any excitement might set them off."

Henri tried to twist out of the grasp of the two priests, but they held on and bore him away. He looked back, but Father Revrony stepped into place directly behind the two priests, and the little boy's frightened face was hidden from view. The three men of the church, with their human cargo, left the house.

CHAPTER 7

Secret Message

Stunned and shaking, Father lunged toward the retreating backs of the priests. Mother caught him.

"No, Paul—no. Not that way. It will do no good. If the dragoons are aroused, there is no telling what they will do."

"But no one can just walk out of the house with my son." Father alternately clenched and unclenched his fists.

"We must think of it as though Henri were going away to school. Don't you remember how we talked about sending both boys to England a few years ago?"

"Yes, but not to a Catholic school."

"There are ways to get him back, Paul."

"How?" Father asked.

"We can give a big gift to the Catholics."

"Buy back my own son?" Father sank into a chair and put his head in his hands. After a moment he looked up. "I'll give them whatever they ask."

"I don't think they'll ask. We must offer."

"Shall I offer the house?" Father asked.

Mother countered with another question. "Don't you have other things—like gold and jewels from Spain?"

"You've known, haven't you? I should have told you all along. Yes, there is a fortune there in the cellar at the pier. I started four years ago to store up jewels in particular."

He stood up. "I'm going to go talk to the judges."

Othalie, the cook, put her hand on his arm. "Monsieur, do not do anything yet. There is another way. Father Revrony is more interested in winning souls than obtaining money. I know beyond a doubt. Do not do anything until I come back."

"But it's night, Othalie. You won't be safe."

"Trust me, monsieur." Othalie ran to get her things.

After Othalie left, Father paced the floor. "I'm going to the port," he said, and left.

"Mother, what's going to happen to Henri?" Pierre asked. "Where will they take him?"

"They'll probably take him to the school near the Catholic church, and they'll educate him there."

"They won't hurt him, will they?"

"No. I understand that the nuns are very kind, but that isn't the point. It's what they'll tell him about God. It will be so confusing. Oh, why can't people worship God as they see fit and let one another alone?"

For the first time since the crisis Mother appeared overcome. She sat in a chair near the kitchen fireplace and was silent for so long that Pierre thought she was asleep from exhaustion. As he drew near to see whether her eyes were closed, she reached out and held him close.

"Mother," he said, "God is a just God, isn't He? That's what Pastor Foudray always says. If people want to do the right thing, He'll help them do it, won't He?"

"Yes, of course He will." Mother stood up, her usual self once more. She began to measure out cereal for breakfast. Later she fretted about Othalie. "Whatever has happened? Where can she be?"

Father echoed the question on his return. Later that night someone knocked on the back door. With a look of relief, Father flung it open, but it was only the beggar.

"Bread, bread, for the love of God, bread." The beggar glanced about the room. "Pastor Foudray and his family have fled to the woods near the estate," he said in low tones.

"Why—why—" Father could only stammer.

A dragoon staggered into the kitchen.

"Bread—give me bread." The beggar droned the words. Mother cut a slice of bread and thrust it into his bands. The dragoon must have remembered that Othalie was in command of the kitchen, for when he saw where he was, he backed out of the room.

"I'll help you get Henri back," the beggar whispered. "They are coming after Pierre next. They'll trap him in some way—make him admit to something they'll claim shows he wants to be a Catholic." The beggar tore strips from the bread and stuffed them one by one in his mouth. He looked at the floor all the time.

"How do you know all this? Why didn't they take Pierre when they were here? Who are you?" Father put his hands on the beggar's shoulders. The beggar lifted his head in a proud gesture, his eyes flashing. Then he slumped back into his former position.

"They took Henri first," he said, answering the second of Father's questions, "in order to put fear in your hearts—the fear that is the very heart of the Catholic Church." His face worked in a strange way that seemed somehow familiar to Pierre. He had seen that look on someone else. He suddenly remembered—Father Revrony.

"Can you help us?" Mother asked.

"I am helping you. Get this boy out of here at once. Tomorrow may be too late."

"If we could only get him to Grand-père's," father said. "But I'm not going to leave you here alone, Mathilde."

"If monsieur trusts me, I myself will take the boy to the estate," the beggar replied.

"Do you know where it is?" Father asked,

"Yes, I have been there many times."

Pierre remembered something else. "Then you were the one that Claude said came the day the edict was revoked."

The beggar nodded.

"Shall I get ready?" Pierre asked his parents.

"Do not take anything," the beggar said. "If we are questioned, it will go very, very hard—maybe La Lanterne prison."

Pierre left with the beggar, after a quick hug and kiss from Mother and a hard handclasp from Father. The beggar glided ahead of him without a sound. Once beyond the garden wall, the beggar stopped and waited for Pierre.

"Keep me in sight. Stay far enough behind me so that if I'm attacked you can hide. Do not try to help me. Your business is to get to your grandfather's. I've written a message for him. I think you'd better carry it."

"Is it on blank paper?"

"Yes."

"Where'll I hide it—in my shoe?"

"No," the beggar said. "That may give you a blister. Can't you hide it in one of the rosettes on your shoe?"

Pierre undid the ribbon and rolled the note in it, tying it in a bow knot.

The walk seemed endless. Fantasies flashed through Pierre's mind. What if the beggar was a Catholic in disguise? What if he took Pierre away from his family forever?

Pierre sighed with relief when he saw the high walls of the estate loom up in the moonlight. Guards stood at the sentry box at the front entrance.

"Well, well," one called out genially as the beggar approached. "If it isn't our old friend—we've been on the lookout for you."

There was a touch of respect in his voice that Pierre did not miss. But there was another tone, too.

"Boys, come here and welcome our guest." The others circled the beggar. Pierre was just ready to run up to him when the guards pounced on the beggar and held him fast.

"Yes, here he is—Francis Revrony—beggar—Huguenot—spy extraordinary. We've caught you at last. La Lanterne is the place for you."

Pierre's heart raced. To learn that the beggar was Father Revrony's brother was shock enough, but Grand-père's men would not act like this. Then in a gleam of moonlight he saw the red coats and blue trousers of the men. They were from the king's army. But what were they doing here? Had they captured Grand-père's estate—and Grand-père himself—and Claude?

The soldiers ordered the beggar to mount a horse. Other mounted men started him back toward La Rochelle.

A heavy hand clamped down on Pierre's shoulder. He felt his knees sag with fright.

"Who are you?" the soldier asked.

"I'm Pierre Le Brun."

"What are you doing here?"

"I came to see Grand-père."

"And who is Grand-père?"

"He owns this place."

"Oh." The soldier turned Pierre's face toward the moonlight. "Well, you look like the old man at that—high cheekbones, long chin. Where are your parents?"

"In town," Pierre said.

Several of the guards came to see what was going on.

"Why didn't they come with you?" the soldier asked.

"Monsieur, if you please—the dragonnade."

The soldiers laughed and slapped their thighs.

"Why did you come sneaking up here in the middle of the night?"

"To tell Grand-père about the dragonnade."

The soldiers burst out laughing again. "He's harmless. Let him in to see his grand-père."

"Search him first," someone suggested.

"Let's see. If you're a spy like our friend the priest's brother, you would have a secret message some place about you," the first soldier said.

Pierre squirmed. Maybe he could kick off his shoe, but that would leave his feet without protection.

The soldiers teased him. "Maybe it's under his lace collar."

"No, in those big patch pockets. No one would think of looking in a pocket," another said, searching. "Nothing there," he said.

"How about those fancy shoes—right under his foot?"

A soldier bent down. "What odd-looking rosettes. He fingered the one with the loose bow. "Well, what's this?"

Someone held up a lantern. "It's a blank piece of paper."

"Young man, is there a secret message on this?" the first soldier asked.

"I don't know, sir," Pierre said.

"You'd better know." The soldier drew out his sword. "Are you afraid to die, little Pierre?"

"I—I don't want to die."

"Then tell me if that paper means anything."

Perspiration dripped down Pierre's back. "Perhaps if the paper were wet—" he said in a low voice.

The soldiers dipped the paper in water. "Yes, here's a message. 'Assyrians are overrunning the people of God.'"

Someone shook Pierre. "What does that mean?"

"I don't know, sir. I don't know."

Pierre held steadfast to his words, feeling new strength. No matter what they did to him, he could not say what the message meant.

"What are we going to do with him?"

"Let him take the message to his grand-père," someone suggested. "These Huguenots have a string of spies from here to court. We'll break this up once for all."

They led Pierre toward the house, past the pond and the well. They took him to the main bedroom on the ground floor. Grand-père sat at a desk, writing. He was clothed in a dressing gown and nightcap. As the soldiers entered, he looked up with a startled expression. At the sight of Pierre, a look of anguish crossed his face. He read the message without a change of expression, and refused to explain what it meant.

"Take him to La Lanterne!"

"No," another said. "I have a better idea. Let's take the boy."

"What?" Grand-père said, standing up. "You wouldn't put a mere boy in that awful prison."

The soldiers appeared pleased at Grand-père's reaction.

"Why not? He's a Huguenot. He was caught carrying a secret message detrimental to the best interests of France. Therefore, he is a spy." The soldier winked at the others. "Just what is the penalty for spying?"

A groan burst from Grand-père's throat. "The message didn't mean anything different from what we all know—that the Catholics are attacking the Huguenots."

"Too late, old man."

"Take me—take me. Let the boy go back to his parents."

The soldier was not through tormenting yet. "Why should we take you? I'm sure the boy will give us all the information the judges need."

"He knows nothing—nothing that would interest you or the judges."

"We'll decide that."

The soldiers led Pierre out. Grand-père followed, but they pushed him back.

"And so, my boy," the leader said in a gay tone, "you are now on the way to join your beggar friend."

Two soldiers mounted horses, and one put Pierre in front of him.

"To La Lanterne," the leader said, and waved goodbye to Pierre with a mocking smile.

CHAPTER 8

Trial for the Innocent

It was dawn before Pierre, half asleep on the jogging horse, awoke to see the tall, grim prison, La Lanterne, with its slits of windows, double doors, and mounted cannon. Soldiers guarded the entrance.

"What brings you here?" the head guard called to the soldiers bringing Pierre.

"We have a prisoner for you."

The head guard helped Pierre down, holding him in a firm grip. "Another Huguenot?"

"Yes. A spy—a boy spy. Can you imagine that?"

The guard studied Pierre. "The question is Where will we put him?"

"What's the matter? Is the prison filled?"

"Last cell occupied early this morning. We'll have to give someone a roommate, but who?"

When the soldiers left, the guard put his finger under Pierre's chin and looked him in the face. "I don't know what children are coming to these days. You look awfully young to be a spy—and a Huguenot, at that."

The guard motioned Pierre toward the circular stone steps inside.

"I think I'll put you in with our latest prisoner," he said.

Pierre started to climb ahead of the guard. After 15 or 20

steps he felt dizzy. When it seemed as if his legs would fold under him, the guard pushed him into a hall. Doors with narrow slits faced the corridor. A plump guard standing by one of the doors jingled a ring of big iron keys at his belt.

"Can you believe it, Tiny?" the first guard said. "This one's a spy."

"The place is crammed full," Tiny said, waving his hands in an absurd, dainty manner.

"When will they have the trial?"

"Oh, tomorrow, or the next day—or next week, or next month. Does it really matter?" Tiny, with a flourish, selected a big key and put it in the lock. The door grated open.

"In there, my little one. Be quick with you."

Pierre stepped into the dark cell. The door slammed shut, and the key grated in the lock. A man in the cell moved a little. Pierre heard the clank of iron, and then as his eyes adapted to the dark interior, he saw that the man was staring out the tiny window. He looked somehow familiar.

Pierre cleared his throat. "Monsieur . . .

The man turned. It was Father.

"Pierre! How did you get here? Did they let you in to see me?" Father hobbled toward Pierre, but a chain around his ankles pulled him short.

"No, I'm a prisoner too." Pierre told his story. "Why did they arrest you?"

"For helping Pastor Foudray."

"But who told?"

"It must have been the mayor," Father said. "I met him when I went to the port last night. He wanted to see the gold goblets again, and he seemed annoyed when I refused. That's all I can figure. He could have seen the pastor come out of the building. I just don't know."

"Father, what will happen to us?"

Father put manacled hands to his forehead. "There's no way of knowing, but I know one thing. If we are freed, we are going to America."

"But, Father, Othalie said—"

"Never mind what she said. Dr. Maurice has had letters from people there. It appeals to me—a brand-new country, where we can start all over. A number of people from La Rochelle have gone to America, and they like it."

A thud at the door startled them both. Tiny thrust in a bowl of watery cereal and a hunk of coarse, black bread. Pierre offered his share to Father, but he refused it.

When Tiny came back later, the food was untouched. He waggled a finger at Pierre. "You, little one, should eat."

"Yes, Pierre," Father said. "You must become accustomed to plain fare."

"Wisely said, monsieur. I understand they are taking the boy first."

"What are they going to do with Pierre?" Father tried to pull himself over to the guard.

"Do not concern yourself about such trifling details, monsieur. Everything in good time."

"But you said—"

"Ah, we must never believe all we hear, monsieur." Tiny passed the bowl to someone outside. "And now, if you will prepare the little one—straighten his collar, run your hands through his hair—"

Father turned a haggard face toward Tiny. "Where are they taking him? Surely you must know that much."

"Really, I must beg you, monsieur, do not agitate yourself this way. We are merely taking the boy to a more convenient spot for a little while—a matter of hours, no doubt."

"You don't mean the—the—" Father choked off the words, a look of horror on his face.

"We won't hurt him, if that is what you mean. No, monsieur, the little one is too valuable for the kind of treatment you are thinking of. Admittedly, in some cases it is very persuasive." Tiny shrugged. "Enough of that. No, monsieur, it is just a matter of a few questions and truthful answers. The little monsieur will speak the truth, will he not?"

"Of course my son will speak the truth." Father stared out the window. "Who are those men I see down there? Are they the judges of the court? Are they having trial today?" He whirled on the guard. "You mean my son will be there instead of me? A boy? Hardly more than a baby, to be questioned by men trained in the law, who know how to twist and turn an innocent statement?"

Tiny looked at his hands and examined his fingernails one by one. Pierre despised being called a baby.

"Father, another boy was questioned like that."

"Eh? Who was that, Pierre?"

"A boy my age."

Father's face showed he was puzzled.

Pierre took a deep breath. "Don't you remember what He said to His parents? 'Wist ye not that I must be about my Father's business?'"

"Of course." Father put his manacled hands over Pierre's head and hugged him. "Forgive me for not understanding immediately. You are my son, and He gave His Son to be persecuted for His name's sake. May God stand by you when you face the judges as He stood by His Son in His trial."

Tiny clicked the key in the lock. "Come, come. This is all

very tender, but the court will soon be in session. We must not keep them waiting. This way, Pierre."

On the first floor Tiny guided Pierre through double doors into a narrow room. Three judges sat in high-backed seats facing the entrance. Tiny showed Pierre a bench to sit on. He himself stood in the aisle with folded arms.

"You have brought the boy too soon," one of the judges said, consulting a paper. "But let him stay. He may learn a lesson here."

A side door opened, and Dr. Maurice entered. His feet were encased in chains so heavy that he could scarcely walk.

"You are Dr. Hubert Maurice?"

"Yes."

"I think we may save time by coming to the point." The first judge talked for a moment with the other two, who nodded.

"Do you admit talking to the Huguenot pastor, Monsieur Foudray, in secret meetings?"

"Yes."

"Did you give him money so that he and his family could leave the country?"

"Yes."

"Are you aware that helping a Huguenot to leave the country is a crime?"

The doctor shrugged. "Yes."

The judge eyed Dr. Maurice coldly and motioned to an aide, who brought some papers to the judge.

"Dr. Maurice, are these papers a history book that you have written?"

"Yes."

"You admit that you wrote it?"

"Yes." The doctor swallowed hard. "I have spent many years

writing it. It will make future generations proud. It is the history of the Huguenots."

The second judge handed a sheet of paper to the first, who examined it.

"Dr. Maurice, is this a letter you wrote to the colony in Boston, Massachusetts? Allow me to quote. 'The country where you live is in great esteem; I and a great many others, Protestants, intend to go there. Tell us, if you please, what advantage we can have there. . . . If somebody of your country would come here with a ship to get French Protestants, he would make a lot of money.'"

"Yes, that is my letter."

"Finally, Dr. Maurice, this court wishes to know if you intend to persist in your religion."

"I do."

"It will be only your obstinacy that makes us send you back to prison loaded with chains."

"In the sight of God," Dr. Maurice said, "I do not persist in my religion because of obstinacy, but because I recognize this religion to be pure, true, and in harmony with the Word of God. I am ready to follow my Savior anywhere He calls me. He gave up everything for me. He died for me. I am willing to suffer anything for Him."

The judge drummed his fingers on Dr. Maurice's history book and said, "The king cannot be responsible for what happens to people who disobey him."

Dr. Maurice said, "I cannot go against my conscience or the Word of God. Do you want me to lose my soul?"

"I don't care whether you lose your soul or not," the judge said. "I want you to obey. For the last time, Are you wholly resolved to persist in your religion?"

"Yes," Dr. Maurice said, "and I trust God will help me always to be faithful to Him."

The three judges talked together for a few minutes. Then the first judge stood up. "Dr. Hubert Maurice," he said, "this court sentences you to the galleys for life. Your history book will be destroyed by fire."

Dr. Maurice swayed as he heard the words; then with head high, he let the guard take him outside. The clatter of the chains around the doctor's ankles sounded in Pierre's ears long after the door had closed behind him.

Pierre was called to the front of the room. He stood facing the judges.

One of the judges said to him, "Did you hear what is going to happen to the doctor for not obeying the laws of his country and for going against the true religion?"

"Yes, sir," Pierre said.

"Do you know what it is like to be sentenced to the galleys?"

"Not exactly, sir."

The judge leaned forward. "Your head is shaved; you are stripped to the waist. One foot is chained to the side of the boat, and you sit with six others holding an oar that is fifty feet long. A man stands over you with a whip, and if you try to rest, he strikes you with the whip. They say a person loses consciousness at the ninth or tenth stroke." The judge sounded as though he enjoyed the description.

Pierre protested. "But I am still a child."* Then his face grew hot. Only a short time ago he had tried to convince Father that he was grown up enough to be tried.

"You are 12 years old," the judge said. "You should have been able to tell the difference between the true church and the false since you were 7. It will be your choice whether you save yourself and your family from punishment. Do you want to be loaded with chains the rest of your life?"

"No, sir."

"Would you like to be exiled to the West Indies?"

"Oh, no, sir."

"Do you love the king?"

"Of course."

"Then you must be loyal. The king wants you to accept the one true church. Are you ready to accept the true church on your own behalf and that of your family?"

Pierre fought down waves of dizziness. He wished he had eaten that cereal and black bread. Then he remembered a Bible verse.

"Sir," he told the judge, "the apostle Paul said, 'Though we, or an angel from heaven, preach any other gospel unto you than that which we have preached unto you, let him be accursed.'"

Pierre felt a surge of triumph as he said the words. Surely the Bible would convince the judges. But they acted as if they had not heard.

"My boy, your family's safety is in your hands. You must decide for the true religion. Otherwise, you and your parents and your little brother must be punished. Speak for yourself and your family. Do you accept the king's church?"

Pierre heard a door open in the back of the room. Running footsteps sounded in the aisle. Pierre turned just as Henri flung himself into his arms.

"Pierre! Here I am! I want to go home."

Pierre hugged Henri. His eyes misted so that he could hardly see. What cruelty made men devise a scheme like this?

No one had to tell him that Henri had been brought in at this moment deliberately to tear at his heart and confuse him on the decision he was being asked to make. Pierre would have to choose between serving God and saving the lives of his family.

----

* In James Freeman Clarke's *Events and Epochs in Religious History,* page 322, this statement is found: "Recently a record was found of a child 12 years old who was sent to the galleys for having accompanied his father to preaching."

CHAPTER 9

Three Days to Flee

Pierre drew Henri down on the bench. A commotion at the back of the courtroom made both boys turn to look. Othalie and Alec entered first, with Pierre's father following. Behind the guards the priest, Father Revrony, came in with an air of disdain.

At the sight of his father Henri jumped up, ready to cry out. Pierre grabbed him. "Don't say anything, Henri. This is danger. Remember our game? We're going to play it now." Henri sank down on the bench.

Pierre tried to make sense of the scene. How had all this happened?

A guard took Othalie before the judges.

"Did you and your husband take this boy from the custody of the church?"

"No—that is, yes. I mean—he was brought to us." Madame Calvet, are you a Catholic?"

"Yes, I am."

Pierre gasped. Othalie was a Huguenot. Why was she denying her religion? But then he knew, and was ashamed. To save his family, hadn't he himself been tempted to deny God? How could he blame Othalie?

"Did you not work for the Le Brun family?"

"Yes."

"And did you call yourself a Huguenot?"

"Yes." Othalie bowed her head and wept.

"Explain to the court how you had Henri Le Brun in your keeping."

"Well, I was home—I mean at the Le Bruns' house—when three priests came and got Henri. Father Revrony was one of them."

"You say, 'got him.' What do you mean?"

"They asked him if he wanted to burn in hell, and when he said no, they said that showed he chose to be a Catholic."

"Yes, very well," the judge said. "By law a child of 7 can choose his religion. And then?"

Othalie straightened in proud defiance.

"I thought of a way to save Henri. I went to the bakery shop and told Alec I was ready to be a Catholic. He took me to the ovens and showed me Henri sleeping on a pile of sacks beside the ovens. Alec said a beggar had brought Henri there. The beggar didn't explain how or anything about it. I went to Father Revrony and told him I would promise to bring up my unborn children as Catholic if he would let me look after Henri. Father Revrony had me sign something, and later he came back and married us."

Othalie looked ready to collapse as she finished her story. The judges talked together, and the first judge pronounced sentence.

"To be a lesson to others, we hereby sentence you for hiding a Huguenot. Your head shall be shaved."

"Oh, no, no! The shame of it!" Othalie whispered, putting her hands to her head. The guards led her and Alec out of the courtroom.

Father Revrony glided up the aisle. He caught Henri's hand and started out with the boy. "I shall now take this child to where he should have gone in the first place—to the convent school."

"Wait!" The cry came with such violence that a hush fell over the room. Father, with clothes mussed and hair uncombed, looked like a wild man as he leaned over the outthrust arm of the priest to reach Henri.

"I will buy back my son. I will give my fortune—my house—my land—everything I own—to the church."

Father Revrony shrugged and attempted to move on.

"Father Revrony," the judge called, "you are forgetting your duty to the church. At least hear this offer."

The priest turned, still holding Henri's hand tight.

"Now, Monsieur Le Brun," the judge said to father, "you know we have ways and means of obtaining this fortune without your consent. You are a heretic, and by the law of the land we can confiscate everything you own."

"Do you wish to try these methods on me?" Father smiled a little.

The judge appeared to weigh Father's meaning. "No," he said at last. "Make your offer."

"I propose to abandon all my possessions, including cargo from my ships already docked, provided my family and I can leave France in safety."

"No!" Father Revrony broke in. "This boy has already made his profession to be a Catholic. The church shall not be robbed of souls for which God thirsts. I have sworn to bring to our Savior the souls for which He yearns, no matter what the cost."

The sound of doors opening made him stop and turn. His mouth dropped open in amazement. The beggar, in his old and dirty clothes, strode down the aisle with vigorous step, completely different from the cringing, stooping figure Pierre had seen on other occasions. Two guards followed.

"My dear brother," the beggar said to Father Revrony, "I suppose I have you to thank for my arrest. We promised to leave each other alone, don't you remember? You were to save souls your way, and I was to save souls my way. Why have you broken your promise?"

The priest's mouth went slack, and he sagged at the shoulders as if a weight had been laid across them. He dropped to a bench, letting go of Henri's hand.

"What is this man to you?" the judge asked, looking from the priest to the beggar.

"He is my brother—Francis Revrony," the priest said.

"But the record shows that he is a spy for the Huguenots."

"That is true," Father Revrony said.

"This court will try him for treason. Are you willing to testify against your own brother, Father Revrony?"

"Yes. I have proof that he has helped hundreds of Huguenots to leave the country. With his heresy he has poisoned all these souls in the sight of God!" The priest ended almost in a shriek.

The beggar looked at his brother and smiled. "You love me very much, don't you?"

"Yes—yes," Father Revrony babbled, losing all control of himself. "My little brother—how could you do this to our mother—to our family? The disgrace—I would rather see you dead; and I will see you dead—before you lure another soul from God. Why do you cling to your heretical beliefs?"

The beggar still smiled in a gentle way. "My dear brother, I have known since childhood that God can be reached directly. We do not need a priest to pray for us. You remember how we used to argue about it." He sighed. "You may bring about death to my body, but you cannot deprive me of the resurrection and eternal life."

The three judges conferred, leaning close together. Presently the first judge pronounced the decision.

"Francis Revrony, for your acts of treason and heresy you shall hang by the neck until you are dead."

"Give me time to pray," the beggar said in a resolute voice, "and I shall be ready to go where God may call me."

The guards led him out the same door that Dr. Maurice had been taken through.

"As for you, Monsieur Le Brun," the judge said, "it is the court's decree that since you have voluntarily exiled yourself and your family, you are welcome here no longer. You must leave France within three days. If you or any member of your family ever returns, the sentence of death will be imposed. And now, Father Revrony, since it is well known that Monsieur Le Brun is a wealthy man, the church will profit by this day."

Father Revrony made a gesture as if to say no wealth in the world could ever make up for the heresy of his own brother.

Father hurried the boys outside. As they crossed the courtyard, Pierre heard someone singing a Huguenot hymn behind the wall that hid the scaffold. Ropes swayed from two tall wooden poles. Even as Pierre stared, the ropes tightened, and at that moment the song was cut off.

A feeling of hatred welled up in Pierre's heart. He wanted to tear down the wall with his bare hands to save the beggar. Questions tumbled through his mind. Why didn't God save the beggar? What kind of God permitted so much suffering on earth? It wasn't fair; it wasn't just.

"He died for what was right, Pierre," Father said, as though he could read Pierre's thoughts.

"Was it God's will that he should die?" Pierre asked.

"It isn't that God willed him to die. He lets individuals choose their own actions and bear the consequences for them. Remember, God promises the eternal future life—not eternal life here and now."

Running footsteps sounded behind them. Othalie, with her shawl over her head, ran up to them, with Alec right behind. The shawl slipped, and Pierre saw Othalie's shaved head. She burst into tears and tried to hide her head under the shawl.

"Othalie, my dear, don't cry. I want to thank you with all my heart for your great risk and sacrifice in taking Henri, and you, too, Alec," Father said. "Now, go with your husband, Othalie. You must not appear to be friendly to Huguenots."

Othalie's eyes flashed with the old fire. "If you think I'm going to leave madame any longer, wearing her fingers to the bone—indeed, I am not. I'll slip into the house as soon as I can." She and Alec went in another direction toward town. Father and the two boys walked home by way of the seawall.

To Pierre's intense relief, when he reached home the dragoons had gone to drill in the town square. Mother was alone. She came to the door wiping her hands on her apron. Tears rolled down her face as she dropped to her knees and hugged Henri.

"Exiled from France?" she said after she had heard their stories. "To be strangers in a new land? How can we bear it? Where shall we go?"

"Mathilde, we are going to America," Father said, and put his finger against her lips as she began to protest. "It is best."

"Why, yes, Paul. I'm sure. We'll have 15 days to get ready—"

"No, Mathilde. We have three days."

"Three days!" Mother sank into a chair by the fireplace.

"All we can take is a bundle for each of us—Henri, too. He will have his bundle to carry."

"I can do it, Father," Henri said.

"We'll have to slip out of here someway without the dragoons knowing. That's going to be a problem. I'm fairly sure that the dragoons at Grand-père's will have moved on by this time. If we can get there, we can sell or trade something for peasant clothes and disguise ourselves. Perhaps Claude can help us."

Mother began to talk as if to herself. "It must be very cold in America. We'll take warm things—"

"Now, Mathilde, I must make clear to you that if we escape with the clothes on our back, we'll be lucky. The first thing for you to do is to sew money on the inside of my jacket—line it with money, in fact."

A voice called from the front door, and Othalie hurried in. She had covered her bare head with a frilled cap that tied under the chin.

"Oh, madame, I will not leave you, no matter what."

When Mother explained that they were going to America, Othalie went white with shock.

"America—of all places! You'd be better off in the galleys—even the West Indies!"

Father stopped her. "The decision has been made. We are leaving within three days. Now we're trying to think of how to slip away without anyone's noticing that we've gone."

Othalie's eyes sparkled with malice. "I know how. I know the very thing. It'll do my heart good to see it." She chuckled in a scornful way. "You know how those dragoons eat—big, fat pigs, every one of them. We'll have a fine banquet for them—bigger than any they've ever had, with plenty of wine. We'll make them all drunk, and then, right in the middle, you go."

Father was delighted with the idea. "Othalie, you're worth your salt. All right, let's get started. We'll have the big dinner tomorrow night."

When the dragoons trooped to the dinner table the next

evening, they exclaimed in delight. There were huge platters of mouthwatering delicacies, pickled tidbits, and enormous jugs of wine. Father kept everyone's cup filled. The dragoons laughed, and drank in high good humor.

At the height of the celebration, each member of the family picked up a bundle of clothes. Othalie watched, pressing both hands against her mouth.

"Now, Othalie, give us just a few minutes; then you go home. Those are my last orders, and I want them obeyed."

Othalie nodded, her eyes brimming.

The shouts of the revelers followed the family well up the road. Mother could not walk fast, and the family rested often. The first streaks of dawn were showing when Pierre saw the outline of Grand-père's walled estate. He looked for the guards at the entrance. There was no one there.

"Father, they've all gone. Aren't we lucky?" A peculiar odor, as of wet ashes, rose all around them. Pierre ran ahead to look. He dropped his bundle in dismay, and a wave of desolation swept over him. Now he knew why there was no one at the gate. Instead of the manor house, jagged black splinters rose to meet the morning sky. Curls of smoke rose from the burned-out timbers. The smell of wet ashes choked Pierre as he blinked back tears. Grand-père's estate had been destroyed by fire.

CHAPTER 10

Trying to Escape

Pierre turned to the others. "Mother, stop," he said, but he was too late. Mother came around a corner in the path and stared at the jagged, broken walls standing black against the sky. She looked numb, as if unable to comprehend what she saw.

"But why? Why would they do this?" She clasped her hands convulsively. "Where's Grand-père? Where have they taken your grand-père?"

She started to climb over the heaps of blackened stone, but Father pulled her back. "Wait, Mathilde. We'll find out everything soon enough. Let me look." His face was white as he too stared at the desolate ruins.

He probed through the ashes with utmost care, sifting and resifting. At last he straightened.

"No—there are no bones here. Grand-père must have escaped."

Two peasants came through the gateway. One was an old man and the other a young boy.

Pierre gave a shout and ran toward them. "It's Claude!"

The old man looked so weak and pitiful, with his trembling hands, that Pierre thought it would be more polite not to ask questions of him.

"Claude, where's Grand-père? What happened to him? Did

you see them set the fire?"

Claude stood openmouthed, looking first at Pierre and then at the old man. "But—"

The old man motioned to Claude to be silent. He took an old hat off his uncombed hair. His face and beard were dirty. His knuckles were grimy. His patched clothes and flapping leggings reminded Pierre of the beggar.

"Well, Mathilde," the old man said when Mother came up, "I'm glad to see my disguise is so good."

"Father, is this really you?" Mother searched Grand-père's face, and then flung herself into his arms. "Tell us what happened—tell us everything."

Grand-père managed a smile. "It's perfectly plain what happened. Claude and I are the only ones left. The others—the peasants—ran away when the fire started. As you can see, I'm a peasant now." He began to chuckle a little. "Yes, thanks to Pastor Foudray, I'm a peasant. Oh, yes," he said, answering Mother's look of surprise, "he's holding meetings near the falls—you know, Mathilde, where we used to go on picnics when you were a little girl. Foudray has quite a system for helping refugees. They have gathered all kinds of clothes for disguises. You'll see some of the Huguenots coming out as pilgrims, or sailors, or beggars, or, as you see me—peasants. This is the first time we've been back since the fire. When was it, Claude?" Grand-père passed a hand over his forehead.

"Two days ago, monsieur—I mean three nights. They started it at night."

"We'd better go find the pastor ourselves," Father said. "It seems to me we'll be safer if we are disguised too."

Claude acted as guide and led the way into the woods at the farther end of the field. Once inside, the group had to go single file. Mother exclaimed as she remembered this or that land-mark—a tree with a twisted root, a special turn in the trail. After they had walked for more than an hour, a murmur like faraway voices reached Pierre's ears.

"The waterfall!" Mother turned her head to listen. "How well I remember that sound." She ran ahead of Claude. "There's the ravine—our secret place." She stopped short. "Why, I hear singing. They must be having a meeting."

A group of Huguenot refugees sat huddled together. Pastor Foudray, his back to the falls, led the singing. He had never looked more vigorous or inspired. He nodded to the newcomers to sit down, and began his sermon.

"In this, the testing, let us turn to the Psalms for comfort. 'Return, we beseech thee, O God of hosts: look down from heaven, and behold, and visit this vine; and the vineyard which thy right hand hath planted, and the branch that thou madest strong for thyself. It is burned with fire, it is cut down. . . . Quicken us. . . . Cause thy face to shine; and we shall be saved.'"

The Huguenot audience responded to the pastor's enthusiasm by sitting more alert. A look of hope replaced the dull fear etched on their faces.

"Our persecutions and afflictions have multiplied," the pastor said. "But how else can we be tested? Shall we sit by our warm fires in our cozy homes and prattle about how true we are to God? No. We are tempted, even as Jesus was tempted. Who of us here has not been faced with the temptation of turning his back on his God?"

At these words Pierre wriggled and stared at the ground.

"We can pray only for the strength to endure. For this reason I would like to change two words in our Lord's Prayer. 'Leave us not in temptation' is what I would say. God will surely lead us out, if we remain true."

After the service the pastor ran forward with hands outstretched and a heartwarming smile on his face. He greeted the newcomers with delight. Father told him that they had to leave the country within three days.

"I can help you," the pastor said. Oh, you should see how our people have been slipping by the guards. Guards are posted everywhere—by every bridge, every fording place, every port. Some of us have hidden in bales of merchandise, loads of charcoal, empty barrels."

It was plain that Pastor Foudray lived every escape and counted each one as a personal victory.

"If you have money, you can bribe a guard."

Father nodded. "I have money and jewels."

"Good. Now, I suggest that you disguise yourselves as a peasant family. We have clothes here. We have everything, including Bibles."

"Oh, may we have one?" Mother asked. "They burned ours." She held the new Bible close.

Pastor Foudray kept talking as he sorted clothes from a big pile. "You can be carrying salt meat to the market. We'll get a donkey." He held up a man's suit. "Madame Le Brun, many of our women have dressed as men."

Mother shuddered. "Oh, no. I wouldn't want to do that. I don't mind being a peasant."

A crashing sound as of underbrush being broken made everyone look up. A band of soldiers swung down into the ravine. The sight made cold chills go down Pierre's back, but Pastor Foudray broke out into a hearty laugh. Had the pastor lost his mind? Pierre looked hard at him.

"Oh, you men nearly fooled me that time." He reassured the refugees. "They're disguised. How did you get these clothes?"

One of the men explained that they had come across a band of soldiers separated from the others and had pounced on them, tied them up, and exchanged clothes with them. In high good humor the Huguenots paraded their uniforms.

The Le Brun family were beginning to look like Grand-père. Father wore shoes tied with colored ribbons, full trousers, long-sleeved shirt, and a large handkerchief folded and draped around his shoulders. Mother wore a full-skirted dress and a large straw hat with a bonnet underneath covering most of her hair. For the first time in his life, Pierre wore the full trousers of a peasant.

Pastor Foudray could find nothing that would fit Henri. He found two baskets made to fit a donkey.

"I think the best solution would be to have Henri sit in one of the panniers, weighted down on the other side to balance him—your bundles, maybe. Remember, you will be taking salt beef to market."

Later, when one of the men brought back a donkey, Father and the pastor showed Henri how he must sit in the pannier with his head resting on his knees. The pastor nodded in satisfaction. "People of every rank have been here—noblemen, scholars, merchants like yourself—and they go out as pilgrims, venders of rosaries, servants, and beggars. Some tell me they have been helped by sympathetic Catholics."

"Like Alec," Henri said. He told the pastor his story. "Are we ready?" Father said afterward.

"One thing more." The pastor picked up a handful of dirt and rubbed it on Father's face and hair. Mother did the same to her face and hands. When everyone had completed the disguise, Claude was the cleanest of all.

"No one will recognize you now." Pastor Foudray laughed

with genuine heartiness. "I suggest that you go back to La Rochelle and board a ship there. If you are questioned, feign stupidity—or even insanity."

The pastor himself guided them back to the edge of the woods. They all knelt while he committed them to the care of God. He left them with one final suggestion.

"Do not follow the road. Stay close to the edge of the woods. A few miles down you will find a hut. It's deserted. You can find shelter there. Watch for soldiers."

The family set out over the rough field. Henri sat upright in the pannier, with the lid back, ready to hide at the first alarm.

Pierre found his wooden shoes clumsy to walk in. In spite of the cold he felt tempted to go barefooted. He envied Claude's easy stride over the rough ground. At the hut the boys coaxed the donkey inside. Only the shell of a house remained. Two rooms had stone floors, and a third one had hardened mud.

While Mother sat and rested, the boys went out and picked up some shriveled apples they found under a tree.

Mother found black bread and cheese that the pastor had packed, and portioned it out to everyone.

"Maybe we should travel by night," Mother said when father put Henri in the pannier ready to travel.

"No," Grand-père said. "It would be unnatural for peasants to travel that way. We must live, eat, and think like peasants."

The family traveled down the coast later in the afternoon. Fishermen were throwing their nets along the low, sandy lagoons and marshes. Across the sea-filled lowlands the island of Rè stretched invitingly two miles away. Guards scanned sand dunes and shallows. When the first soldiers loomed into sight, Pierre's pulse quickened.

"Father, there they are."

"Move slowly. Don't look at them. Henri, you must stay down. Your life depends on your being quiet."

"Father, I can do it," Henri said with a smile. "I've played that game lots of times with Pierre." He wriggled into a comfortable position, and Father, with Grand-père's help, fastened the pannier lid tight.

Pierre, alert to every new sight and sound, pulled at Father's arm. "Look at all the ships in the channel, Father. Aren't there more than usual?"

"Yes. Those are the king's ships. They must be searching every vessel for Huguenots."

The soldiers did no more than look casually at the travelers, and the family moved onto the pier itself not long after. Market carts rumbled past, but the crowds of a few days ago had dwindled. A number of dragoons on horseback patrolled the length of the wharf.

"What providence this is!" Father pointed to a ship. "There's an English vessel I recognize. I didn't expect it here for another week." He led the group to some stone steps leading to the water. "We'll watch for the English captain himself."

Boatload after boatload of sailors came ashore, and finally the captain came, elegantly dressed from shining boots to wide-brimmed, plumed hat.

In a low whiny voice Father began to chant. "Salt beef for sale, fine salt beef."

The captain ignored him and mounted the steps.

Father took a step after him. "Salt beef . . . sir, your assistance. I am Paul Le Brun."

The English captain gave a start of surprise, faltered, and halfway turned. Pierre could not hear what Father said, but the captain strode on, with father a step behind.

94

In a few minutes Father returned. "It's settled. He will take us to England. All we have to do is to find a small boat someplace and get to the ship's side someway. From then on we will be safe."

"Paul," Grand-père said in a warning voice. Pierre saw a dragoon on horseback approaching.

"Beef—salt beef for sale," Father said in a low, guttural voice.

The dragoon rode up close. "What do you have in these panniers?"

"Salt beef—for the market. Would you like some?"

Pierre tried to hide a gasp of fear. Why had Father said that? What if the dragoon wanted some?

The dragoon made a face. "I don't like it myself." Before anyone could move, he whipped out his sword and thrust it into the nearest pannier—the one where Henri was hidden.

"Good luck at the market," the dragoon said, as he drew out his sword. "Did you say salt beef?" He held out the sword. The tip was red with fresh blood.

CHAPTER 11

Surprise Voyage

For a moment no one moved. There was neither sound nor movement from the pannier.

The dragoon smacked his lips. "That's more like it. Fresh beef. You'll have no trouble selling it." He sheathed his sword, wheeled his horse around, and rode away.

Father and Grand-père lifted the panniers off the donkey and carried them partway down the stone steps. With gentle hands they pried the lid off. Henri, with a proud smile, straightened up.

"My leg's bleeding. Something sharp stuck it, but I didn't cry out once, did I?"

The sword had grazed the calf of his leg. Mother tore off a bit of cloth from the bundle in the other pannier and bound the wound.

Footsteps sounded near the steps. The English captain, with an expression of surprise, started down.

"My son," Father explained. "Monsieur Captain, do you think we could go aboard now? My son is wounded." Father handed him money. The captain waved it away.

"I do not dare take the chance. It isn't safe. Our ships are subject to searches without notice. I shall sail tomorrow and will pass between the islands of Rè and Oléron. If you can come out in a small boat, as I explained, that will be the safest way. I'll take you aboard as soon as I am sure the custom-house officers are through."

"Could we arrange a signal?" Father asked.

"Hoist your sail and let it fall three times. I'll do my best to get you aboard safely."

With the arrangements made, Father placed Henri in the pannier again, and the group traveled down the seawall a few miles until they came to the mud huts of fishermen. Father and Grand-père selected one and knocked at the door. A woman came out, closing the door behind her.

Father offered money. "We would like to stay here for the night."

The woman looked at the money and into the faces of both men.

"Runaway Huguenots, are ye?" She spoke in a matter-of-fact voice.

"Yes," Father said.

"Well, come in, come in, all of you—and the donkey, too. It would be mighty suspicious to leave him outside. I don't want any questions from those snoopers." She tossed her head in the direction of the beach.

Pierre expected to see some show of surprise when Father lifted Henri out of the pannier, but the woman watched with arms folded without a flicker of expression. She looked as if nothing would surprise her.

The woman showed them a dark corner inside. "You can stay there."

There was no flooring in the hut. Both Pierre and Claude tripped over something.

"It's a man!" Claude whispered. Snores rose from the floor. "He's asleep." He tripped again and held out a warning hand to Pierre. "Here's another. Why, the place is full of sleeping people!"

"Been walking all night," the woman said in explanation.

"They're from Marennes. Who are you people?"

Father lowered Henri to the floor before he answered. "I'm Paul Le Brun. We're from here in La Rochelle."

The woman's face lighted up. "Monsieur Le Brun! To think my small house is so honored. Here, let me clear out some of this trash." She bustled about, pushing fishing tackle and wooden tubs aside. "My husband is on your boat fishing for cod in Newfoundland this very minute. I never dreamed you'd ever step inside our house."

From the way father relaxed, Pierre knew everything would be all right. They could trust the fisherman's wife.

She pointed to the other visitors. Pierre counted six.

"Look at those two men," the woman whispered.

Pierre made out two slight figures.

"They're really women dressed like men. What do you think of that? I helped them cut off their hair. What you poor people have to go through to escape! Now, what are your plans?" she asked Father and Grand-père.

Father explained. "Do you know where I could hire a boat and a pilot for tomorrow?"

"Indeed I do. My own young brother will take you. He loves the excitement of all this. But you'll have to go tonight. It's the only safe way."

When it was dark outside, the other refugees left two by two, with their hostess' advice as farewell.

"Avoid the high roads—and if you get caught, pretend you're dumb, or insane." She handed out road plans to each group. "An old beggar left these with me," she said. "He asked me to give them out as long as they last." She excused herself and left.

In a little while she came back with a young fisherman. His ruddy face glowed with excitement.

"Leave everything to me, gentlemen. We'll take the shallop and skim around those ships of war like a bird."

Father paid the woman and left her the donkey.

"I don't know how I can explain this donkey to the tax collector," she said, a tone of doubt in her voice. "But I'll think of something." She shooed it into a corner of the hut where her worktable stood and tied it fast. "Goodbye, Monsieur Le Brun, and good luck to you."

At the shallop the young fisherman directed the group to lie down on fishing nets. He hid them with an old sail.

"I've got to avoid the pinnaces. They're everywhere. Now, you try to go to sleep, and in the morning I'll drop anchor near the English ship and cast my nets."

Every little while the fisherman called out in a husky whisper, "Passed that one. They didn't suspect nothin'."

The hours passed. Pierre did not even try to whisper to Claude or Henri. He dozed and woke a dozen times.

"There she be!" The fisherman's cheerful tone startled Pierre completely awake.

"Don't show yourselves. It's morning. There comes a king's frigate. It's signaling the English ship to anchor."

The fisherman kept up a running commentary on what he could see. "The officers are boarding. . . they're signaling to sail." Then he groaned in dismay. "The ship's sailing away!"

"Run the sail up three times." Father spoke for the first time. "That's the signal."

"It's dropping anchor at the other end of Oléron," the fisherman said. "We'll catch up and signal them."

Later Pierre heard the fisherman running up the sail. "There," the young man said. "They saw it. Now all we have to do is wait until it's dark."

At nightfall the shallop pulled close to the ship. When it was his turn to climb the rope ladder, Pierre felt as if his arms and legs had turned to water. It was good to feel the solid deck beneath his feet.

Father paid the fisherman, who whistled in appreciation. "But I'd have done it anyway," he said. "I like lots of excitement." He pushed the shallop back from the ship and turned toward shore.

"Welcome aboard," a genial voice sang out in French.

Pierre stared. This was not the English captain but a French one! His eyes were close together. His crooked teeth gleamed in a grin as he swung his lantern high and eyed the refugees.

"Where is the English captain? I have business with him," Father said.

"Monsieur, I am afraid you have mistaken my poor little ship for one belonging to our good neighbors across the channel. I am afraid you will have to make the best of it for some little time. You see, my orders were to sail when the wind was favorable." He shrugged. "It is quite favorable, as you can see. But I don't mind this slight delay. I'm always glad to pick up a few passengers. Perhaps you would like to see your quarters."

"But we haven't booked passage on this ship!" Father took a threatening step forward.

"Stop, monsieur." The French captain beckoned to some of his crew standing nearby. "I would regret having to restrain your tendency to move indiscreetly."

The ship moved steadily out into the bay all the time. Where could it be going?

"My men will show you the hold. Perhaps after seeing it, you might wish to make arrangements for better quarters for your family. It could be done." The captain raised his eyebrows in a meaningful look.

Two crewmen took them to the hold of the ship and showed them a rope ladder. "Down there's where you'll be unless you have money," one said.

The air was close and fetid, with the odors of human bodies. Mother stumbled and leaned on Grand-père. She held a handkerchief to her face. The only light came from a lantern in the hatchway where the rope ladder hung, and Pierre could see that Mother kept her eyes closed. He could hear groans and heavy breathing from below.

"Are you one of us?" a woman's voice called. "Are you Huguenots?"

"Yes. Are you prisoners? Are there many of you?"

"Yes, we are prisoners. There are 57 of us."

Pierre could see the outlines of people half lying, half sitting on thin mattresses. The flickering lantern cast shadows as it turned with the movement of the ship, and Pierre was not certain whether he was really seeing people after all.

"What is your crime?" Father hesitated on the word, for he knew well they had not committed any crime.

"We will not worship the beast, nor fall down before images. That is our crime." It was the woman speaking again.

Another fervently called out, "We entreat you to remember us in your prayers. Ask that God give us grace to persevere to the end, that we may have a crown of life." A man's voice came clear. "All things come from Him who is the King of kings. It is in Him that we put our trust."

Other voices assented.

"It has pleased God to call us to suffer, even unto death, for His holy name," another woman said. "God has been very good to us in enabling us to bear up under trials of every kind."

One of the Huguenots began a hymn. The others joined in.

At first their voices wavered; then they grew strong, until they sounded joyful.

Several of the crew, cursing, brought tubs of water to the hold. They pushed the Le Brun group aside and tossed the water over the people. The singing stopped. The crew took the Le Brun family back to the captain.

"I'll let you think this over for a while, and you can let me know if you wish the accommodations below." He walked off.

One of the crew looked at the group for a moment or two. "Where are you going?"

"America."

"Why do you want to go there?"

"To be free." Father's tone was curt.

"Free?" The seaman snorted with laughter. "The miseries that await you in America will make you wish you were back in France with a good king. Don't you know that all men are hanged if they refuse to attend Mass, and women are slaves for the savages?" He slouched away.

"Father, what is America really like?" Pierre asked. "Why do people go there if it's such a terrible place?"

Before Father could reply, the French captain came back. "How do you like our ship, monsieur?"

"It's beastly and inhuman. I have means," he added in a lower tone. Grand-père gave him a warning look.

"I thought so, monsieur. Your clothes did not fool me. Your voice, your accent—they were those of a gentleman. These means that you mention—of what do they consist?" the captain asked.

Father took him aside and pulled out a leather pouch. Pierre and Claude strained to see what was in it.

"It's jewels," Pierre whispered.

The French captain raised his voice. "That will be fine, monsieur. I shall see that you are well provided for."

"But I want the others down there provided for too. These jewels are worth a king's ransom, and you know it."

The captain's tone was soothing. "Of course, of course. Everything shall be attended to. Just leave these matters in my hands. monsieur. It is a pity, this whole distressing incident. Of course, you realize you will not need money where we are going?" Again his voice was questioning.

"Where are we going?" Father's voice was tense.

"What? Didn't the Huguenot missionaries tell you?"

"No."

"Regrettable. It may come as a bit of a shock." The captain's polite murmur died away and he showed his crooked teeth in a wide smile. "This vessel has been ordered to sail to the West Indies."

If a death sentence had been uttered, the effect on the group would have been no greater.

CHAPTER 12

Strangers No Longer

S tunned and silent, the family went to the cabins assigned to them. The night seemed endless. Pierre dozed and woke. He could tell that Claude and the others were doing the same. Some-one shook his shoulder.

"Wake up. Make no noise. We are leaving the ship."

Father woke each one up, and in a few minutes the family stood on the deck, ready to descend a rope ladder. The night was cold. Spray hit everyone. Pierre felt Henri trembling on one side of him, and he could hear Claude's teeth chattering.

After a few more minutes they were all in a small boat. Father exchanged a few words with the man on watch, and when he reached the boat he took up the oars and pulled with all his might away from the ship.

"We're near the coast of England," he said, panting. "I bribed the seamen." He could not spare the breath to say more.

Dawn began to break, and Father headed for a curve of the shore. Pierre and Claude took one oar. Grand-père offered, but he was too weak to hold a steady course.

The moment the boat landed, Pierre jumped out, elated. "We're free!"

Everyone cheered up, and laughing and talking, the family headed for a group of fishermen who could be seen on the shore. From then on, time and events streamed by. The fishermen passed the family on to some of the village folks.

"London," Father told everyone. "We want to go to London." Everyone was sympathetic.

"Huguenots," they whispered. "They're refugees." Their glances were respectful.

Father found money changers, and with the help of shop-keepers and an innkeeper, the family was able to clean up and put on English clothes. At last they set out for London in a coach. Everyone was carefree and lighthearted.

London puzzled Pierre. There were the same narrow, crooked streets as he had seen in France, but in London the houses looked fresh and substantial. Public buildings were going up on all sides.

Father explained why. "There was a great fire here 20 years ago. It destroyed nearly the whole city. Now they are building with brick instead of wood." The three boys were entranced with the coffeehouses and cookshops along the way. Father hurried them along. He pointed to a sign hanging over an inn. A minia-ture sailing ship in full sail was painted on a board hung by chains to a crossbeam.

"Wait here." Father went in and came out with a beaming, ruddy-cheeked Englishman.

"The name Le Brun is an honored one here," the innkeeper said in French with a quaint accent. "Leave everything to me."

In a little while the Le Bruns were installed in rented rooms. The innkeeper brought over several other French Huguenots.

"Oh, yes," one of the visitors said in answer to Father's ques-tion, "I've been here for years. Did you know we have two French Protestant churches here? And did you know that for French refugees who have no money, the English people raised a fund—five years ago, I think it was—for their relief? It's known as the 'Royal Bounty,' but I don't think the English king approves. It should be named the 'English People's Bounty.' Not that you would be concerned, for you do not have this problem."

The kindness of the English people was almost overwhelming. In a few weeks Father had a position similar to the one he had had in France. Once again he was concerned with ships and sailings. He said no more about America.

But in late April 1686 he came home dispirited. "We are going to America."

"Why, Paul, whatever has happened?" Mother asked.

"It looks as if the old persecution will start anew. Jean Claude, a banished Huguenot pastor, published here in England an account of the Huguenot persecution. The French ambassador complained." Father was silent.

"Yes, Paul?"

"There is to be a public burning of his book on May 5. The people here are Protestant, and they are our friends. But the king is a Catholic. And don't you see—the same thing is about to happen here in England as it did in France. Gradually advisers may persuade the king to take stricter measures, and there we'll be, in the same situation as before. We are going to America."

"Father, may we see the burning of the books?" Pierre asked later.

"Yes, I want you to remember in later years why we left a country whose people have been so good to us."

When the day came, the whole family went to the square. A crowd of silent Englishmen watched men build a fire. The public hangman brought out copies of the book and threw them into the blaze. A ripple, almost a groan, passed through the group of watchers.

An old man near the Le Bruns shook his head. "What a pity!"

His English speech was strongly marked with a French accent. Grand-père spoke to him in French. The old man turned in amazement.

"Why, yes, I was a Huguenot pastor—from your country. Marennes, to be exact."

Father showed interest at once. "Had you ever planned to go elsewhere? America, for example?"

"No. England has been good to me. Do you mean you're thinking of going to America?"

"Yes."

"Don't go, my friends, don't go."

Father pointed to the fire. "Isn't that reason enough?"

"But the persecutions in France will abate. Louis XIV will surely alter his policy toward the Huguenots. For myself, I hope to preach again in France before I die." Seeing that Father was determined, the old pastor added, "if you insist on going, you must see Robert Thompson. He's a London merchant of high standing, and he is president of the Society for Promoting and Propagating the Gospel Among the Indians. See him. He can give you all the help you need."

Robert Thompson was most enthusiastic when he heard Father's plans. "The General Court of Massachusetts has given me 500 acres in the Nipmuck country. It has also granted eight miles square as a tract for settlement, provided 30 families occupy the land and provided an orthodox minister accompanies them. Your boys will enjoy America, I'm sure," he said, smiling at the three.

The family worked at fever pitch preparing for the trip. On sailing day Pierre exclaimed in astonishment. Sailing vessels with upthrust masts covered every inch of the Thames River. It did not seem possible for any of them to move an inch, but the Le Bruns' ship soon nosed into the open sea.

At first the novelty of being on the ship kept the three boys busy from morning until night. Then as days and weeks followed, Pierre could hardly remember any other way of life. The journey was pleasant until the last few days, when a heavy storm came up. With Boston Harbor in sight, the ship was unable to dock. Below deck the passengers tossed and tumbled, but no one was really alarmed until a ripping and roaring sound combined with the crash of waves and thunder.

The captain, white-faced but resolute, hurried to warn the passengers. "The ship has struck a rock. Everybody on deck. Don't wear too much clothing—you may have to swim."

Rocks loomed high ahead. The ship listed sharply. A horrible crunching sound joined with the wind. The last Pierre remembered, he was fighting for breath and being banged against the rocks.

Pierre choked and sputtered. The boom of waves receded. Salt prickled his eyelids and stung his nose. His hands hurt. He looked at them in surprise. They were scraped raw where he had clung to a rock.

At first he could react only to one sensation at a time. His ears roared. He shook the water out. His hair lay in a wet mass over his forehead where a wave had flung it like seaweed. He coughed. A few feet away, someone echoed his coughing. Pierre looked up and saw Claude.

The storm was over. Farther on, Henri sat by Grand-père, crying. Pierre crawled toward him. Claude followed, and the three boys propped Grand-père against a rock. His head had dropped back and his face appeared peaceful, almost smiling.

"Why doesn't he open his eyes?" Henri asked. "Why is he smiling like that?"

"Any survivors?" a strange voice hoarse with worry called out.

"Yes, thank God," another answered.

Small boats landed. Men jumped out and ran along the beach looking for the passengers. Pierre found Father and Mother conscious, but too weak to stand.

The people of Boston opened their homes to the refugees, and after the count was taken of the survivors, it was determined that among others, both Grand-père and the old Huguenot preacher had drowned. There were not enough people to settle the Nipmuck country, and Father decided to settle in Boston. Within a few months he was once more in a familiar position, dealing with ships and cargo, and Mother was in charge of a snug, warm house.

The three boys learned everything they could about their new country. There was nothing to fear from the savages in Boston. Wild animals were far off in the woods. As for food, the three boys learned to love corn in short order.

Claude took it on himself to learn how the land was tilled. He prepared the earth carefully, planting corn, perhaps four or five kernels at a time. Pierre and Henri helped, but already Pierre liked to be on the wharf watching ships come and go with their cargoes of furs, timber, fish, and cloth.

One day Father came home with a letter. "It's from La Rochelle." He opened it and began to read to himself. As he read, his face whitened; then a slow flush started from under his collar and crept up his cheeks.

"Why, whatever is the matter, Paul?" mother asked.

"Why, why—" Father could not do anything except sputter.

He waved the letter. With a sudden, angry look, he tore it into shreds and threw it into the fire. Then he burst into laughter. Tears of merriment poured down his cheeks. When he recovered, he explained. "That letter said I'm to appear at the door of the Catholic church in La Rochelle on October 7 and show cause why my lands and property should not be confiscated."

He paced the room. "I'll write a letter back." He seized pen and paper and sat down to write. Mother and the three boys remained quiet.

Afterward, Father flourished the letter and read it aloud. "To Whom It May Concern: 'Every one that hath forsaken houses, . . . or lands, for my name's sake, shall receive an hundredfold, and shall inherit everlasting life.' We shall never forget how we have fled from persecution and found acceptance before the people of this land; how, when we were strangers, they have taken us in." He handed the pen to Mother. "We'll all sign this."

Afterward, he took the boys with him to the wharf.

"This letter is going back on the very next ship."

He arranged with a captain to take the letter. The captain was curious and asked Father many questions about his new life in America. Then he turned to the boys.

"Do you like living in America?"

"Yes," they chorused.

"What do you like most about it?"

Claude spoke without hesitation. "There's so much land for crops."

"How about you?" the captain asked Henri.

"Nobody has to hide in America."

Pierre hesitated before giving his answer. Somehow it seemed important to define and express all that had happened to him in the months that had followed the revocation of the Edict of Nantes. He wanted to say, "No one burns up your home. No one puts you in prison. No one tells you how to worship God." Somehow he could not get started.

"Well?" the captain prompted.

"The nicest part about America," Pierre said, "is that the people here let you live the way you want to. They take you in as friends, whatever your religion. Back in our home country we were treated like strangers in the land. Here we are strangers no longer."

OTHER EXCITING STORIES
IN THE FAMILY FAVORITES SERIES

THESE WATCHED HIM DIE
Leslie Hardinge
They were there that day—
they saw Jesus die. And
these are their stories.
Paperback.

THE SWORD OF DENIS ANWYCK
Maylan Schurch
Paperback.

THE GATES SERIES
by Thurman C. Petty, Jr.

SIEGE AT THE GATES
The Story of Sennacherib,
Hezekiah, and Isaiah
Paperback, 160 pages.

THE TEMPLE GATES
The Story of Josiah,
Jedidah, and Judah's Idolatry
Paperback, 144 pages.

FIRE IN THE GATES
The Story of Nebuchadnezzar,
Jeremiah, and Baruch
Paperback, 112 pages.

GATE OF THE GODS
The Story of Daniel, Nebuchadnezzar,
and Loyalty to God
Paperback, 128 pages.

THE OPEN GATES
The Story of Cyrus, Daniel, and Darius
Paperback, 176 pages.